THE ACCIDENTAL GOD

Copyright ©2014 by Arlene F. Marks
All Rights Reserved

No part of this publication may be reproduced or transmitted in any form or by any means, electronic or mechanical, including photocopy, recording or any information storage and retrieval system without the written permission of the author and publisher, except by a reviewer who may quote brief passages in review.

Disclaimer
All characters in this book are fictitious, and any resemblance to actual persons, living or dead, is purely coincidental.

Cover Design: M Kleiber

Author's Photograph: M Kleiber

Library and Archives Canada Cataloguing in Publication

Marks, Arlene, 1947-, author
    The Accidental God / by Arlene F. Marks.

Issued in print and electronic formats.
ISBN 978-1-927890-04-2 (pbk.).--ISBN 978-1-927890-05-9 (pdf)

    I. Title.

PS8561.R2868A62 2014	C813'.54	C2014-905355-X
		C2014-905356-8

Printed in United States of America
Published by Sun Dragon Press Inc., Canada
www.sundragonpress.com
First Edition, 2014

Best wishes only!
AFMarks

THE ACCIDENTAL GOD

BY

ARLENE F. MARKS

Sun Dragon Press Inc.

DEDICATION

Dedicated to the memories of Thorne Smith and Edwin A. Abbott, whose stories provided the inspiration for this book.

Dedicated also to my talented sons, Robert and Chris.

ACKNOWLEDGEMENTS

In the many years that it has taken this story to grow into a novel, I've been helped by a host of people.

Thank you to all the editors who sent me fan mail rejection letters and whose publishing houses would have accepted my book if only it had been a little longer and a little more serious.

Thank you to the friends and family members whose comments and reactions after reading drafts of this novel have deepened my insight and broadened my perspective, in particular David Marks, Bette Walker and Jodie Schaefer.

Thank you to the many teaching and writing colleagues whose friendship and encouragement have kept me on my feet and optimistic. Of special note: Debra Hanff, teacher-librarian and book-lover extraordinaire; Ed Greenwood, always busy but never too busy; Julie Czerneda, a generous spirit; and George Scithers, who may be gone but will never be forgotten.

Special thanks to Marilyn Kleiber, my remarkable publisher. Much have we suffered together, and much have we learned. Tennyson's Ulysses would have been proud.

CHAPTER ONE

If he had a mouth, Demonai would be smiling.

He wasn't actually a 'he', of course, any more than Tillah was a 'she' – their kind came in just one model – but the soft outline and gracefully undulating approach of his fellow being always reminded him of a threedee female wearing a long flowing garment. The curiosity now rippling through her essence was all Tillah, just as the disapproval radiating in waves from the being following her was the natural state of Olla'set, their aggregator. Tillah and Demonai had each sparked to life inside one of his collection sacs and he never passed up an opportunity to remind them of it.

Olla'set extended a communication pod for melding. Enjoying the other being's evident impatience, Demonai purposely delayed before extending one of his own.

What are you doing with that?

With what, Aggregator?

With that bubble of five-dimensional space you just submerged to the core of your essence. Did you remove it from my collection sac?

Not at all. I found it.

Of course, you did. In my collection.

Respectfully, Aggregator, you're mistaken. This bubble couldn't possibly be part of a collection, since it already contains sentient life.

Olla'set's shock, like everything he felt when communicating, was punishingly palpable. *In five-dimensional space? Impossible!*

I've been studying these creatures. They perceive three dimensions and can imagine those with higher numbers. They strive and question. They plan and make choices. What further proof do you need of their sentience?

They are my creations. Any sentient being can create life in lower dimensions, Demonai, but only the Universe itself can bestow sentience upon aggregated matter, and only beings of the highest order are capable of receiving it.

As if simply claiming ownership and quoting doctrine would persuade Demonai of anything. The Universe had clearly been in a contrary mood when it ignited his aggregated essence.

Beings like us, you mean?

Of course, beings like us! Sentience would never be wasted on creatures incapable of perceiving all the dimensions of reality, declared Olla'set. *These life forms—*

I call them threedees.

A fitting name for a plaything. These threedees cannot even perceive all the dimensions of their own limited reality. Therefore they cannot possibly be sentient regardless of how they behave, and I want you to stop wasting your time with them.

I won't let you disaggregate them, Olla'set.

I have no such plans for them. You misjudge me, Demonai.

Tillah finally joined the meld. *Then what are your plans for them, Aggregator, if you wish Demonai to abandon them?*

Demonai knew from experience what the response to this question would be, what it always was when Olla'set perceived a challenge to his authority. The aggregator's essence sparked fiercely, then went ominously still.

So, you are together in opposing me?

It was a question, Aggregator, nothing more. I am curious to know how you plan to dispose of this dimensional bubble if Demonai is not allowed to keep it.

Tillah and Demonai had often cooperated to test Olla'set's patience in the past. But her demeanor at this moment was mild, even conciliatory, despite the provocative nature of her communication. Demonai couldn't help wondering whether she had plans of her own for the fascinating inhabitants of the rocky accretion inside the bubble. Had she known perhaps, even before Demonai did, that Olla'set had them in his collection?

All right, then, here is my decision. Since you are so enamored of life forms in five-dimensional space, Demonai, I hereby command you to compact and confine yourself – all of yourself – to the first five spatial dimensions. You will be contained inside the bubble with your pet creatures for as long as it takes you to come to your senses and admit that our kind are the only truly sentient beings in the universe.

Olla'set had returned to normal, for Olla'set: radiating self-righteousness as he issued edicts. *Tillah, you will be the bubble's guardian for the duration of Demonai's captivity. You may insert a pod at intervals to check on his condition. When the threedees cease to amuse him, I am confident he will beg to return to fully dimensional space.*

It took a huge effort for Demonai to delay his glee until after the meld was dissolved. Olla'set had no idea, could not even imagine, how much fun he had just sentenced the 'captive' to have.

CHAPTER TWO

2003

March 15, 3:45 p.m.

"April fool."

James Hollinger eyed the brown folder his assistant, Stewart, had just dropped in front of him. "April doesn't start for weeks. And what the hell is this?"

"The Harrington-Smythe account."

"Harrington-Smythe? I thought Elliot Brooks was taking care of them."

"He was. They fired him...again. The Misses Harrington-Smythe say they're tired of being passed from partner to partner in this firm. They want no one less than the Great Man himself handling their assets," Stewart announced with a wicked grin.

Hollinger scowled darkly for a moment at the file, which occupied his desk blotter like a rectangular coffee spill that refused to be absorbed. "Terrific," he growled, and wiped a hand across his forehead. He would rather have been wiping the smirk off his assistant's face.

Stewart had no idea what it was like having to deal with a couple of *really* old maids on the prowl. Euphonia and Iphigenia Harrington-Smythe. Even their names were ancient, for God's sake. They refused to do anything electronically—everything had to be face to face. The last time they'd cornered Hollinger in his office, they'd leered at him for a solid hour, giggling obscenely behind liver-spotted hands. Months later, the memory of being mentally undressed by a couple of oversexed octogenarians still made his skin crawl. If the sisters hadn't been old money, with solid-gold social connections, he would have referred them to a competitor long ago.

"Who's got the lightest load at the moment?"

Stewart didn't even have to look it up. "Kurt Jessup, but not for long. Tax time."

"It's long enough. Drop this folder in Kurt's basket, with a note: terribly busy, about to go on vacation...you know the drill."

"He'll send it back, you know, with another note." Stewart's grin had broadened. The kid was having altogether too much fun with this, Hollinger decided. If he'd thought he could slip it past the other three partners, he would have promoted Stewart to account manager, body piercings and all, just for the pleasure of watching *him* deal with the 'weird sisters'.

"Then it'll have to sit for a while. I won't be here."

"Right. Your private clients."

Stewart's face pinched a little, with either envy or disdain, Hollinger wasn't sure which and certainly didn't care. Strippers made good money in this town and they filed annual tax returns, and a few of them still happily paid his fee to ensure that they got back every penny of rebate they had coming.

"They were my first walk-in customers, Stewart, when I had the storefront. They helped to launch this company. I'm not going to abandon them just because our current clientèle live in mansions and own entire towns."

"That's so kind of you, boss, letting those poor women come to your home to spare them the embarrassment of having to walk into this sumptuous office. And if they decide to show their appreciation in, shall we say, nonmonetary ways...?"

Hollinger nearly laughed. Show their appreciation? Hardly.

Twenty-five years ago, it would have been a different story. They'd all been a lot younger then. He could have had any one of those girls, any time he wanted. Like a fool, he'd held back. He'd had goals. He'd had integrity. Mainly, though, he'd had a lousy self-image. Lord, what he wouldn't give to be back in his twenties, knowing what he knew now! It wouldn't matter what shape his body was in – despite the claims made by ads for workout equipment, what women considered most attractive in a man were tangible assets, earning potential, and a healthy investment portfolio.

Then, as now, the field would have narrowed to one: Roxanne. Still the fairest of them all, she had long ago set her sights on a third career, as the wife of a very wealthy man. She made no secret of it, and he didn't care. Once a year, they played house in Hollinger's penthouse suite while he did her tax return.

Roxanne's paperwork was a disaster. Sometimes it took the entire first week just to organize her receipts. But her assets made it all worthwhile. Hollinger glanced at his watch. In just another few hours, sweet Roxanne would be putting those delectable assets in his hands.

He could hardly wait.

* * * * *

"Garry, I wish I had something good to tell you."

Doctor Garrick Boehm shifted uneasily in his chair. He hated these meetings. His supervisor at the project, Dr. Dunberry, always came back from budget conferences with bad news for him. Boehm was acutely aware that his branch of the research was the most recently undertaken, and that in the event of a budget cutback he would be the first to lose equipment and funding. In five years, Dunberry had never once missed an opportunity to remind him of his tenuous position.

"What do I lose this time?" he sighed, running a nervous hand through his shock of sand-colored hair.

"All of it."

"What?" Boehm frowned incredulously at his colleague. "You mean I'm off the project? Fired?"

Dunberry shook his head. "I wish it were just one person. But our grant has been canceled, so the whole project is being shut down. The government is trying to cut back its spending and this theoretical type of research is considered expendable right now, and – Hell, why am I justifying this?" Dunberry sighed. "Some short-sighted mandarin pulls a plug and seven years of work goes down the tubes. We're done. They've given us seventy-two hours to turn over all our findings so far. Then we vacate the facility. Garry, I'm so sorry about this. Most of us have jobs waiting for us in the private sector, but you were recruited straight out of university."

It went against everything that he was feeling inside but Boehm shrugged and mustered a resigned smile. Money, he thought sourly. Everything in this world boiled down to money – the people who needed it and the people who had it. Somebody with money had decided not to share it, and now he was out of a job. Just once before he died, Boehm decided, he wanted to know what it felt like to have that kind of power over other people's lives.

"Listen, Garry, why don't you go to your office and clear out your things? We'll do all the compiling and organizing for you. It'll give you extra time to look for another position. How about it?" There was a pleading expression in Dunberry's eyes. Boehm could almost believe that the old man was feeling genuinely sorry for him.

"Terrific, thanks," he murmured, getting to his feet.

As he made his way through the labyrinth of corridors to his closet-sized office, Boehm reflected that the years he'd spent on the project hadn't been a total waste. Being constantly starved for resources had sharpened his ingenuity. And his meetings with

Dunberry had trained him in many bureaucratic skills, such as acting humble while being stabbed in the back.

At last he was able to close his door on the world and settle his rangy body into the hard wooden chair behind his desk. His computer with the monitor perched atop it sat like a desert island in a sea of paper. A random tumble of printouts and hand-scrawled notes and carelessly dropped file folders, it was—appropriately, considering his current situation—a rather choppy and unfriendly sea. He was probably the only person in the building who could make sense of it. And Dunberry expected him to be packed up and gone by nine o'clock the next morning.

With a sigh, Boehm began to sort through the clutter, discovering several broken-backed texts he'd used for reference and then forgotten to reclose. Many of the books on the battered metal shelf unit behind him had been borrowed from the university library. A few he'd brought from home. He would have to find and label a couple of boxes to pack them in. And what about the files on his computer? He would have to go through the hard drive, deleting anything personal, maybe e-mailing it to himself first or transferring it onto a memory stick.

There was a reason that moving house topped the list of stressful life experiences, he reflected glumly. It could take him all night to bring order to this chaos.

Well, what the hell? It wasn't as though he had to get up early to go to work.

* * * * *

Fingers poised over the keyboard of her laptop computer, Claire Amory scowled fiercely at the screen with its margins so precisely yet tactfully delineated in baby blue. Toolbar icons sat obediently awaiting her attention. The cursor pulsed patiently in the upper left corner of the page. And her mind, which should have been buzzing with story ideas, was just as empty of words as that clean white screen.

Damn!

She hadn't been able to write anything in over a week. It felt like an eternity. Bills were coming due and her savings were dangerously depleted. If Claire couldn't break through this infuriating block and send off at least three short pieces to guaranteed markets, she would have no choice but to accept one of Ralph Ignace's freelance editing assignments, just to meet the next rent payment.

Editing porn. Unbidden, a line popped into her head: "It's a dirty job, but somebody's gotta do it." Yeah, she thought disgustedly, it sure was.

Three years earlier, low on funds and desperate for any kind of writing work, Claire had answered an ad in the newspaper. She was from a small town. She was still learning how to get around the city on public transportation. How was she supposed to know that pornographers placed want ads just like everyone else?

Claire sighed and leaned back in her folding bridge chair, reminding herself for the umpteenth time that success in the writing business wasn't a question of talent, but of luck. Even editors who had rejected her work agreed that she was a good writer, sure to find a large readership if she could just 'mate her style with the right subject matter'. The way Claire's luck had been running lately, that would probably turn out to be porn.

Three and a half years. Long enough for a scientist to make a Nobel Prize-winning breakthrough. Long enough for a computer nerd with marketing savvy to become a multimillionaire. Apparently not long enough for a small-town girl to rocket to writing fame in a city boasting at least twenty publishing houses. It hadn't been for lack of effort, either. Since arriving in Toronto, Claire had made more acquaintances than she could count, but only two real friends.

One of them was Ralph Ignace, the pornographer with the

proverbial heart of gold. He was constantly praising her writing ability; and he always had work for her when she needed it, and never held back a payment on her. The other was Sophie Hopper, vice-president of Women for Professional Equity. If she ever found out that Claire was cashing cheques from Pussyjoy Enterprises, there would probably be hell to pay.

Not for the first time, Claire thought about Caverley Corners and the job she had left there, managing the counter in Mister Bowmeister's dry cleaning establishment. A secure little job in a secure little town. Maybe that was her problem, she mused. Too much security and not enough experience. She'd thought there would be a magical transformation in her life when she moved to Hogtown, as Toronto was called by many rural Ontarians. Not a very complimentary nickname for the largest city in Canada. Surely a provincial capital deserved something better, she thought, something with the word 'big' in it. New York was The Big Apple. New Orleans was The Big Easy. So what was Toronto?

Claire had thought that success would be hers for the taking here; sadly, she'd been wrong. The expedition to the big city had so far been a bust.

The Big Bust. Perfect. And she probably had Ralph Ignace to thank for the twist of perspective that now enabled her to conclude every creative thought with a sexual *double entendre*.

Well, it was time to stop being creative and start being practical. Claire needed money. That meant she had to write and sell a really great story. A first-person account of some kind of adventure. Something unique and exciting, that other people would want to read about. Nothing heavy or too strange. Just something that she could slant to several national publications to increase her chances of acceptance. A sale to a major magazine would pay the next couple of months' rent and buy her some breathing space.

So, this would be a story about...what? What was she qualified to write about besides growing up in a small town and following her dreams to the big city?

At once the answer came to her. She nearly gagged on it. Then she thought, Well, why not? She'd been editing the stuff for years. And Pussyjoy was making money hand over fist, so somebody had to be buying it, right?

Claire straightened in her chair and, gritting her teeth, began striking keys in ever faster rhythm.

CHAPTER THREE

Tillah did not wait long to pay him a visit.

How can you bear it, Demonai, being confined to such a small space?

It's spacious enough for your entire essence to join me here, he invited.

Only in a severely compacted state. Thank you, but no. And what is that constant vibration?

That's the threedees communicating with one another. They generate wave patterns. Would you like to know what they're communicating?

The location of food? The presence of danger?

Do you honestly believe I would have stood up to Olla'set on their behalf if that was all the threedees were about?

She paused, the essence in her pod shimmering. *You don't believe he actually created them, do you? You're certain he must have found and collected them, to play with. You took a great risk, Demonai. He could have disaggregated you on the spot for stealing them from his collection sac.*

I never admitted to stealing them, he reminded her.

No, you just turned his attention from your transgression to his own: Thou shalt not stuff another sentient being into thy collection sac. Tillah's amusement sparkled like tiny stars. *So, are these threedees meeting your expectations?*

If you mean are they sentient, the answer is yes. If you mean are they intelligent, however...

Don't be too hard on them, Demonai. Their existence is limited to three and a half dimensions, and they've been at Olla'set's mercy ever since he acquired them.

And he's shown them none. He's played his cruel games with them over hundreds of their lifetimes.

And how does this reflect on their intelligence, exactly?

He made no effort to conceal his disgust. *They're worshipping him. They think he's a god. Tillah, he's disaggregated them by the thousands and they've made sacrifices of their own offspring to appease him. And their belief is so strong that when I began communicating with them in an effort to undo some of his damage, they called me an evil spirit and tried to drive me away.*

You found a way to communicate with them? Her pod glowed with excitement.

I had to, in order to study them. Monitoring is the easy part. Let me show you. First, you extend a pod and compact it down to three dimensions, then pick a spot and push—

Like this?

Her eagerness was explosive. Her first attempt flattened fifteen square miles of boreal forest. Her second displaced a thousand tons of ocean water, raising tides that drowned fishing villages on multiple coastlines. Demonai took over then, showing her how to compact and refine her pod for precise transition through the fourth dimension, then decompact it for implantation into a three-dimensional object, all without causing so much as a single wave of disturbance.

There was more he wanted to teach her, about moving and changing coherent matter and infiltrating the containment membranes of the threedees, but it could wait. She'd made progress, and he knew that Tillah's curiosity would bring her back to learn more.

They spent a while monitoring the communications of the threedees, which for Tillah right now were nothing more than random vibrations. Not surprising. It was her first time. Demonai was confident that, like himself, she would eventually learn to interpret and even generate the threedees' wave patterns.

No wonder Olla'set was drawn to this bubble. There are bundles of coherent matter all through it, she observed.

Yes. The threedees are apparently collectors. (*Like us,* he nearly added, but stopped himself. Tillah wasn't the one he most needed to persuade.)

Collectors? How interesting! Of what?

Of all sorts of things. Things that they find and things that they make. Some of them even collect other threedees, constructing places to contain them.

And is there a goal to all this collecting? When the sac is filled, do they aggregate its contents to critical mass, then detach it and start over?

Some of them do. Threedee reproduction is the next thing I plan to investigate, once my current experiment is concluded.

Your experiment?

Everything was compacted in fifth dimensional space. Positioned closer to Tillah's containment membrane than would normally be tolerated, Demonai could feel his essence quivering in sympathetic response to her sparkles of amusement. She already shared his belief that the threedees were sentient, but clearly there was something else he needed to persuade her about.

Yes, my experiment. Observe.

Demonai! What have you done to these poor creatures?

I'm granting their wishes. Or rather, I'm letting them grant one another's wishes. This one has power but wishes for youth, this one has an uncertain future and wishes for power, and this one has youth and wishes for an uncertain future. I've melded their essences in fifth-dimensional space, creating direct sensory-motor pathways between each wisher and the being who possesses what he or she wishes for.

Are you telling me that these threedees asked you to do this to them?

Not exactly. They wished for youth and power and excitement, all three at the same time. I simply chose the best way to answer them.

And they can't feel the meld? It causes them no discomfort?

None at all. They have no idea they're linked. I am curious to observe how the threedees react when they realize that they're both getting and not getting what they want.

CHAPTER FOUR

2003

March 16, 8:03 a.m.

James Hollinger opened his eyes and saw...purple. Ceiling, walls, door, all the same ghastly color. This wasn't his bedroom – unless someone had crept in during the night with a can of paint and vandalized the place. Or else – no, it wasn't possible!

The Harrington-Smythes had once joked about having him kidnapped aboard their yacht and taking him on a pleasure cruise. ("Pleasure, get it?" Wink, wink. Nudge, nudge.)

Shivering with trepidation, Hollinger raised his head and looked around. He was alone. The light filtering through the pale gauzy curtains cast no bar-shaped shadows on the wall above the bed. That was encouraging. And he could feel that his wrists and ankles weren't bound. Good. Unless there was muscle waiting for him outside the door, all he had to do was find something to wear and get the hell out of there.

Hollinger flung aside the blanket, swung himself out of bed—and sat, staring helplessly, choking in sheer disbelief, at a pair of legs that couldn't possibly belong to him and yet were clearly attached to his body. They were slender and hairless, and they emerged from the lacy hem of a short blue nightgown.

His heart was pounding – it sounded like drums in his ears – and an icy fist was jammed inside his chest, making it difficult to breathe. Desperately, he looked around the shabby little room and saw a folding bridge table with matching chair, a battle-scarred chest of drawers with a cloudy mirror stuck to the wall above it, and a tea kettle sitting on a hot plate in what appeared to be a kitchenette in the far corner. He was definitely not aboard the Harrington-Smythe yacht. So where was he? More to the point, *what* was he?

The mirror. The mirror would show him.

He should have closed his eyes while getting to his feet. Instead, he noticed the hand on the end of his right arm and fell back onto the bed in shock. The hand was slim and graceful, and adorned with red nail polish.

Tentatively, he felt his cheeks. No whiskers. And not just smoothly shaven, but gone, totally!

"Oh, my God! Oh, shit!" His breath was coming in ragged gasps now. With an apoplectic shudder, he groped the place where his dick ought to be.

Nada.

Suddenly his throat felt hot and tight. Tears were welling in his eyes. His stomach was doing flip-flops. There was a waste basket beside the bridge table. Reaching as far as he dared, he managed to hook the rim of the basket and pull it toward him, not a moment too soon.

A while later, he lay back against the pillows, sniffling and hiccoughing and waiting for the last vestiges of nausea to pass.

Hollinger knew it would be traumatic, but it was even more important now that he look at himself in the mirror. Somehow, wobbly legs carried him across the room, where he stood for a long, silent moment, blinking, and clinging to the dresser top, and trying his damnedest not to pass out.

The face he now wore wasn't unattractive. It was heart-shaped with cupid's-bow lips, uptilted nose and wide blue eyes. And it was young – mid to late twenties. If he had to be the butt of some cosmic joke, things could have been much worse.

He could have ended up in Iphigenia's body. Or Roxanne's.

Then he would have awakened to the sight of...what?

Hollinger went cold all over. What *would* Roxanne see when she woke up this morning? His corpse? Or his body, with someone else's mind in it? This woman's mind?

His imagination chose that moment to leap ahead, showing him the damage that could be done by two hysterical females to an expensively-appointed penthouse apartment.

Dear Lord, he had to get over there!

* * * * *

Garry Boehm was having a very strange dream. He was sunbathing nude on a pale soft beach under the unreal brightness of a midday sky, and a beautiful naked girl with large breasts and dark flowing hair had just sliced off his left arm at the shoulder with a wicked little knife. But instead of blood, perfume was spilling from the wound and evaporating into a thick, aromatic mist that billowed around him like smoke. Finally he coughed, sending the dream spinning off in tiny fragments and catapulting himself into another one much like it.

He was still nude, but lying on a huge bed. The blue sky had folded itself around him, becoming walls and a ceiling. The strong smell of perfume remained in his nostrils. And there was a voluptuous naked woman, with blond hair and dark roots this time, sleeping peacefully on a left arm which logic dictated must belong to him, but that he couldn't feel at all.

Boehm needed that arm. Sitting up, he held the woman still with his right hand and pulled himself free. And then she opened large brown eyes, smiled languorously up at him and stretched. Suddenly a smooth hand was snaking across his shoulder to caress the nape of his neck.

He really had to marvel at the vividness of this dream. He was even experiencing the pain of returning circulation in his arm.

"Darling," came a silky voice beside his left ear, "I want you."

If he needed any further proof that he was dreaming, mused Boehm, this was it.

"I said, I want you," she repeated, her breath fairly melting his eardrum.

If she'd popped out of his subconscious, then she had to represent something. Perhaps she was symbolic of the resentment he'd felt when Dunberry told him the project was canned...?

The woman's hand had left his neck and was walking on fore- and middle fingers down his chest. He stopped it as it tried to leap over his navel. "I'm analyzing," he told her.

"So analyze," she replied with a smile. "It isn't your brain I'm after, anyway, darling."

He glanced downward.

So, it was *that* kind of dream.

Boehm sighed happily and leaned back against the pillows. "Oh, yeah, baby," he murmured.

* * * * *

Claire Amory came soggily aware, conscious at first only of pain. She could feel that her body was unnaturally bent, which probably explained why every muscle in it was aching. Eyes shut, she took rapid inventory. Her head was pounding. And her mouth tasted like a swamp. And her breath smelled like one. And her tongue –

She didn't want to think about her tongue.

Claire hadn't felt this bad since she'd let Ralph talk her into a second glass of punch at the Pussyjoy office Christmas party.

Was that where she was? Because she sure as hell wasn't in her own bed.

I will stay calm. I will stay calm. Even if I've been drugged and kidnapped and thrown into a steamer trunk, I will not dissolve like some weak female victim, she told herself sternly.

Then she opened her eyes and had to clap a hand over her

mouth to keep from screaming. And then she realized what she was feeling with her hand and yanked it away from her face as though she'd just touched a hot stove.

Whiskers?

Claire blinked hard several times and gazed around the room. The overhead light was on, had probably been on all night. The place was furnished like an office, but it felt more like a cell. It did have a door, with a small window in it. And an old-fashioned keyhole, the kind they used to have in dungeons. The sight of it made her stomach churn.

Carefully, she unfolded herself from behind the desk. It was a very small room, scaled-down as well as narrow. Claire's heart fluttered like a trapped bird as she stepped slowly toward the door and reached out for the knob.

I will stay calm... I will stay calm...

The door opened – *thank goodness!* – into a corridor with whitewashed cinder block walls and a double row of doorways leading away in each direction. Down the hall to her right, she saw a washroom sign and, with a sigh of relief, headed towards it. Once her most pressing need was taken care of, there would be time to deal with the rest.

Or maybe not. Claire saw herself reflected in the mirror over the washbasin and nearly screamed again.

What had been done to her?

Gone was the heart-shaped face framed by straight dark hair. The one she now wore was indisputably masculine. It stared back at her from under disheveled dark blond hair, its lean angular cheeks sporting a day's growth of beard. Its eyes were dark and deep-set, its expression twisted with horror.

Where was she? Who was she? Who was *he*? And where—?

Stupid question. Claire knew exactly where he was – waking up in her body, in her little bachelorette, and probably terrified out of his mind.

Frantically, she began searching her pockets. Men didn't carry purses. They had wallets. If she was lucky, this man would have enough cash on him to pay for her cab ride home. It was an unaffordable luxury, but so was the time she would lose riding public transportation.

Aha! His name was Garrick Boehm. And...he had no driver's licence. Nothing with an address on it at all. Damn! If he'd already panicked and run off, she would have a hard time tracking him down.

Sophie, she thought grimly, *you'd better be wrong about men being the weaker sex.*

Claire jammed the wallet back into her pocket and hurried into a stall. Garrick Boehm's bladder was ready to burst. And she had a body to catch.

CHAPTER FIVE

Tillah's essence went utterly still. *So you're playing games with the threedees? Tricking and tormenting them? Tell me again how you and Olla'set are so very, very different from each other.*

I don't disaggregate them for my own amusement.

And you're certain Olla'set does?

Did. You may be its guardian, but the bubble belongs to me now, and I...grant...wishes.

Yes, Demonai, you're a god among the threedees. But not a good god, according to them. An evil spirit. A deceiver. So why would any of them ask you for a favor?

I don't know. They just do. Shortly after I discovered the threedees, I was monitoring the activity at a gathering place, and I implanted a pod in a carved figure that a threedee had placed outside his shelter. A short while later I observed a young female threedee being attacked by a group of males. The threedees who witnessed the event called her names and did nothing to help her. When the males finished abusing her and left, she crawled over to the carved figure and used it to pull herself back up onto her feet. And she was praying to any god who would listen to avenge what had been done to her.

And you were listening, and angry, no doubt. Did you disaggregate them?

Worse. I terrified the entire gathering place. I prepared several more pods and waited for the same group of males to approach the female again near the carved figure. As she observed, I lifted the males into the air, then let them fall to the ground. And I vibrated the matter of the carved figure to make sound, and warned all the threedees in the area that this female was never to be harmed again or they would be answering to me.

You told them your name?

Well, I couldn't let Olla'set take the credit, could I? After that, things just spun out of control. My communication had disaggregated the carved figure, but it was immediately replaced with another larger one. Females began to come, alone and in pairs, with prayers and offerings. Then the owner of the figure traded it to another threedee with a large collection of females, and they all made prayers and offerings. Then the threedees built a separate shelter to hold the figure, and next thing I knew, threedees were migrating from other gathering places to visit it.

With prayers and offerings, of course.

I couldn't ignore them, Tillah. Those females...the other threedees treated them so badly. If you had been there, you would have protected them too.

So Demonai became a god by accident. Does it ever occur to you that perhaps the same thing might have happened to Olla'set?

Briefly. Then I remind myself about all the threedee offspring who have been dropped into the sea or thrown into volcanoes or left on mountaintops to die, in his name.

Are you sure about that? she persisted. *Do they actually use his name? Because, like you, if I wanted to take credit for something, I would make certain others knew what to call me.*

Demonai considered fiercely for a time, his essence sparking with the effort required, but he finally had to admit, *I have never heard Olla'set's name spoken aloud by any of the threedees I've monitored.*

As Tillah withdrew her pod, Demonai remained still, remembering. The abused female had called out to many gods for vengeance, not just one. In the restless whorl of dimensions that filled this bubble, all constantly rippling and eddying like excited essence, somewhere she was still calling out. Threedees were drowning and burning alive and being blasted to bits by the changes Olla'set had made to their world, the floods and tremors and exploding mountaintops. Demonai couldn't place a pod in the third dimension without sensing the threedees' terror and feeling them scream for mercy to a whole collection of strangely-named gods, none of them answering—and none of them Olla'set.

If he had communicated with them at all, they would have known what to call him. But they didn't. So he clearly hadn't. And why should he, if he truly believed they weren't sentient?

Purpose began taking shape at the core of Demonai's essence. Somehow, he had to get Olla'set inside this bubble and put him in communication with the threedees. Only then would he believe what Demonai already knew – that sentience was possible in five dimensions, and no matter how enjoyable it might be to interfere with the threedees from a distance, their sentience made interacting with them—and especially conspiring with them—a lot more fun.

CHAPTER SIX

1967

March 26, 9:45 a.m.

"Slattery, you are *such* a loser."

With a sigh of agreement, Rick Slattery slid over on the sofa as his friend and roommate Cormac O'Toole dropped down beside him. Mac exhaled noisily, then gazed around the living room, grinning with bleary satisfaction. "Some bitchen happening we had, eh?"

Rick did not respond. They had hosted a pre-exam party last night for nearly fifty people, and he had been awake for an hour already, glumly assessing the damage.

Snack food littered the apartment like bomb shrapnel in a war zone. Someone had overturned a full bowl of popcorn on the coffee table, then walked away with the bowl. Peanut shells, pretzel sticks and cheese twists had landed and stuck in puddles of spilled beer that had been left to dry, turning the hardwood floor into an obstacle course for bare feet.

Not all the guests had been total slobs. The Engineering students had thoughtfully erected pyramids of empty beer cans on nearly every horizontal surface. Someone had left a leaning tower of pizza cartons beside the front door. And the faint aroma of weed hung in the air, no doubt as a friendly reminder to mellow out.

"That chick was so hot for you, man. How did you manage not to score? No, never mind, I already know the answer." O'Toole shook his shaggy head in disgust. "I worry about you, man. This is supposed to be the best time of your life, and instead you walk around as if the weight of the world is on your shoulders. Do you have any idea how good you've got it? Your uncle is the dean of the law faculty, all the profs know it and give you chance after chance, and time after time you keep blowing it. Don't you want to be a lawyer? 'Cause if you don't, you need to point yourself in a different direction, *ay-sap*. I'm serious, man. You need to learn how to have fun. I'm your best friend, and hanging out with you lately feels like I'm watching a slow motion train wreck."

"Are you done?" Slattery inquired wearily.

"That depends. Are you listening?"

"Yes. Are you? If I don't get my law degree and pass the bar, I'll be breaking a tradition that's been part of my family for ten generations. Nobody cares whether I actually practice law. I just have to graduate from this faculty at this university. So that's what I'll do, whatever it takes."

"Does your family realize that you're struggling just to pass your first year courses? Or don't they care about that either?"

Slattery shrugged.

"Well then," sighed O'Toole, getting to his feet, "here's my suggestion to you, my friend. You take that antique lamp or gravy boat or whatever the hell it is that you found at the flea market in Wasaga last weekend and rub it a few times, and hope that there's a genie inside who can help you get through the next four or five years of your life with both your health and your sanity intact. Meanwhile, exams are looming, so if anyone is looking for me I'll be working my ass off to qualify for another fun-filled year at this prestigious institution of higher learning." He paused and sniffed the air. "Higher being the operative word in this case," he added. "I'd open a window if I were you. You know what they say about the effects of second-hand toke."

"So you're leaving me to clean up? Again?"

Mac surveyed the living room and made a sour face. "You're right. Call in the groupies, man. This place is too disgusting for either of us to touch."

Mac was the one with groupies, the one with the Gibson guitar and the semi-famous folk rock band. Mac had also been blessed with broad shoulders and easy charm and beer-ad good looks. Rick was the sidekick, the one with the forgettable face and fade-into-the-woodwork nature and nothing better to do than be a sounding board for other people's brilliant ideas – when he wasn't busy keeping the apartment habitable and worrying about flunking out of school. Living proof that opposites did attract, Mac and Rick had been close friends since high school, the force of nature and his shadow.

Sometimes Rick got depressed enough to wonder why someone like Mac would even associate with him. Sometimes Rick's father even wondered about it, aloud. At those times, Rick and his mother would lock eyes in silent commiseration.

That was why he had bought her the lamp for her birthday. Antiques were her secret pleasure. Even though the one he'd picked up at the flea market was probably just a mass-produced replica, he knew she would appreciate the thought.

Richard Slattery Senior, meanwhile, had taken his wife on a European tour for her birthday, so the gift from their son would have to be sent to their hotel in Paris. Rick went to his bedroom to prepare the lamp for mailing. As he unwrapped it from its cocoon of white tissue paper, however, his heart dropped. He'd forgotten about the tarnish. Or maybe it was just dirt. Whatever it was, it lay in dark blotches all over the spout of his mother's birthday present. With a sigh, Rick cradled the lamp in the crook of his left elbow and rubbed experimentally at one of the spots with his other shirt sleeve.

Hey, Ricky, let's have some fun.

Slattery froze in mid-wipe. Hardly daring to breathe, he stared uncertainly at the lamp. Had he really heard that?

Come on, the voice coaxed, *you know it's what you really want.*

"Mac, that isn't funny, man," he called out.

There was no reply. Slattery dropped the lamp back onto the tissue paper on his bed and went to find his friend, but Mac had gone out. Slattery was alone in the apartment with the owner of the voice. No, he amended, his heart racing after a rapid and thorough search of every closet in every room, he was just alone in the apartment, period. And hearing a voice as clearly as if someone were standing right beside him.

"I'm going crazy," he murmured.

No, Ricky, you're not. I'm Demonai. I live in this lamp. And if you seriously want to have the best time of your life, don't tell Mac about me.

"Trust me, I won't be telling anyone about this, because you're not real."

The voice chuckled, raising gooseflesh all up and down Slattery's arms.

Test me. Make a wish.

"You're kidding." Rick's voice came out an octave higher than usual. He hadn't paid much for the lamp. Perhaps he ought to drop it in the nearest dumpster and just send his mother a card for her birthday this year.

I'm serious, Rick. You can wish for anything except lasting harm to another living being.

Those last words, a direct quote from Professor Lindhurst's most recent lecture on ethics, instantly halted Slattery's stampeding imagination. He'd been right the first time. Mac was playing an early April Fool's joke on him. If he looked carefully enough, Rick would probably find a camera and a speaker hidden in his bedroom. And hadn't Mac made a point earlier of telling him to rub the lamp and hope for a genie?

All right, my friend, Rick decided. You want to play? Let's play.

"Okay, Demonai. The apartment is a sty. Clean it up."

Done. Walk into the living room.

Slattery strode through the doorway of his bedroom and found himself standing, speechless, in the middle of a scene straight out of a Disney film. Every room of the apartment had been invaded by glowing white orbs about six inches across. They darted and spun in all directions, like a pillaging army of overweight Tinkerbells. Wherever they paused, something disappeared in a bright flash of light. The pyramids of beer cans, the pile of pizza cartons, the peanut shells and cheese twists that had been sat on and stepped on and trodden into the carpet, even the butts in the ash tray, all blew up and vanished before his astonished eyes. When the orbs had finished their work, they shrank to points of light which all winked out in unison, leaving the apartment cleaner than Rick had ever seen it.

This was impossible. It was insane!

"Holy shit..." he breathed, suddenly finding breathing itself difficult.

Is that real enough for you, Ricky?

The voice was right behind him. Slattery spun around and found himself staring directly at a pale, pulsating ball of light hovering just a couple of feet away, and his heart nearly stopped. The orb was blocking the path to his bedroom – an ominous sign – but it also didn't seem to be making any move in his direction. For at least thirty seconds he stood as though frozen, never taking his eyes off the thing. Then he blinked, and it was gone.

"How –? How did you –?" he gasped.

Not important. What you need to keep in mind is that I'm on your side. Hey, man, I'm offering you the opportunity to have fun, to have groupies, if that's what you want. You can be the main attraction. Mac can be your sidekick for a change. What do you say to that?

It sounded wonderful, which meant there had to be a catch. Slattery had grown up reading stories about supernatural beings that offered to grant wishes, so he knew enough about genies to be wary of this one. Willing his breathing to return to normal, he replied carefully, "I like it, Demonai. It's just – This is a lot for an ordinary human to take in all at once."

Listen, I understand. You need time to digest what's just happened. That's cool. When you've figured out what you want me to do next, just rub the lamp. Oh, and next time...? No more parlor tricks, okay? Make a real wish. Revenge is my specialty, by the way. Tell me who's pissed you off lately and I'll help you get even. It'll be fun.

Yes, it would be fun, he suddenly realized.

"One question, Demonai: What did you do with all the garbage you removed from the apartment? Is it vaporized or something?"

Nope, just collected. I can put it back if you like. Or I can disaggregate it. Whatever you wish.

"Actually, there is somewhere I'd like you to put it."

* * * * *

Sitting on his bed, legs outstretched, with the lamp perched on the pillow beside him, Slattery waited, gleeful anticipation growing like a bubble inside his chest. Shortly after one o'clock, he heard the apartment door open and close.

"Hey, those groupies did a great job," exclaimed Mac's voice from the living room. "They worked fast, too. What did you promise them? Whatever it is, I'm up for it, man."

Slattery said nothing, just glanced at the lamp and grinned. He heard Mac's footsteps travel from the living room to the kitchen, and then to the hallway outside Rick's door. He imagined Mac reaching for the knob of his own bedroom door and had to clap a hand over his mouth to avoid spoiling the surprise.

"Rick, are you hungry, man? I have to grab a clean shirt and get back to the stacks, but I brought you something from the hamburger joi – Hey! What the hell?"

With that, Rick's merriment could no longer be contained. It blew his hand off his mouth and poured out of him in howls of uncontrollable laughter. A moment later his door flew open and Mac stalked in, struggling to keep a stern expression on his face.

"Rick Slattery!" he exclaimed in mock indignation from the foot of the bed, sending his friend into even more spasms of hilarity. Mac grinned, then chuckled indulgently. "This was brilliant, man. Did you do it all by yourself?"

"I must confess," Rick managed to reply between guffaws, "I did have a little bit of help."

"Uh-huh. Well, I'm glad you finally decided to have some fun, my friend. It looks good on you. By the way," he added on his way out the door, "your lunch is somewhere in my bedroom. Happy hunting."

Once Mac had left the apartment again and Slattery's laughter had subsided, Demonai commented, *Let me guess – you want me to find that hamburger?*

"No, thanks. Just take out the garbage. Vaporize it this time, please. Or whatever it is you do to get rid of stuff permanently."

Your wish is my command.

Recalling the expression on Mac's face as he entered the room, Rick couldn't keep himself from giggling.

You really enjoyed playing this joke on your friend, didn't you?

"I did. I haven't had that much fun since..." He fell silent, instantly sober.

... since before your father sat you down to have a serious talk about your future?

Rick stiffened. "How do you know about that?"

I sort of eavesdropped on your conversation with Mac earlier. It was a logical guess. Besides, I have some personal experience in this area.

"The Slatterys are a special breed, son," said Rick, quoting from memory in a poor imitation of his father's measured baritone voice. "You have greatness in your genes, and some very large footsteps in which to follow. We're confident that you'll do something memorable with your life."

Memorable, Demonai repeated. *There's some wiggle room there. Did he say* how *he expected you to be memorable?*

"I've always assumed he was talking about changing the world. Becoming a political leader, or a captain of industry, or a Supreme Court justice. Something lofty. Something impossible," he added wistfully.

Why would that be impossible?

"Because in order to change the world Slattery-style I first have to graduate from law school, and right now I'm not sure I'll even be able to do that."

All right, then, let's forget about doing it Slattery-style. How would you like to be the most memorable law student ever to walk the halls of this venerable institution?

"And how would I do that exactly with a grade point average of two-point-four?"

How long do you think it will take Mac to forget about the joke you played on him today?

"I don't know. A long time, I guess. Wait, Demonai, are you suggesting—?"

Not suggesting, Ricky. Recommending. Urging. Prescribing.

"But how is playing pranks on people going to make me memorable, except to the people I play the pranks on?"

These pranks won't just be played on people. They'll target the institution itself. The administration. The professors. All the self-important beings who reside on the pompous plane of existence. You aren't the only one whose life they delight in making difficult. Trust me, your classmates will adore you. Even your victims will secretly admire you.

"Right. How about the police? Will they secretly admire me too?"

The police won't be able to touch you, because you will have an ironclad alibi every single time.

"Then how will anyone know that it was me?"

Oh, they'll know, Ricky. They just won't be able to prove anything.

Slattery grew thoughtful.

"Keep talking, Demonai."

CHAPTER SEVEN

When Tillah next appeared, Demonai was ready for her.

I've decided you're right, Tillah. I have been too hard on Olla'set. But he's still mistaken about the threedees.

You must be enjoying your captivity, then. Olla'set won't even consider releasing you from this bubble until the two of you agree.

I'll prove to him that the threedees are sentient. Then we'll agree.

Or, you could lie to him, tell him that you've come around to his way of thinking.

And then he would replace the bubble in his collection and go on tormenting these creatures without once trying to actually learn about them. And when his sac became full, he would aggregate the matter in it and wipe them all out of existence. I'm sorry, Tillah. I can't allow that to happen.

You care about them that much?

I understand them that well. In some ways, they're very similar to us.

For example?

Let me show you.

Demonai had anchored himself to several carefully selected locations which they would be visiting in sequence.

What is this gathering place? Tillah asked once they were implanted at the first stop on the tour. *Or is it a collection container?*

The threedees call this a hospital. Beings come here to be repaired. Observe, Tillah. This female's collection sac has reached critical mass. She is about to expel a new threedee.

Interesting. She has a number of sacs inside her membrane, moving matter back and forth. But where is her essence?

Demonai had been waiting for that question. *Right there. It's coherent matter, like everything else in three-dimensional space. The threedees carry their essence in a special pod.*

But what happens when they retract the pod?

They don't. Threedees are expelled with all their pods already extended and that's the way they remain.

If their essence occupies such a small area inside their containment membrane, then perhaps Olla'set is right about these creatures.

He is wrong, Tillah. If you or I were that tightly compacted, we would occupy about the same amount of three-dimensional space.

And those other collection sacs? What do they do?

I'm not sure, but I do know that each one has a purpose, and they're all inside her for a reason.

Really? Observe how the female is struggling to expel the aggregated matter. This is not a very practical arrangement, Demonai, Tillah declared. *Sacs belong on the outside of the containment membrane.*

The threedees are made very differently from us, it's true. Observing them has made me wonder what a higher-order being might see if it were looking at us.

According to Olla'set, there are no higher-order beings than ourselves in the universe.

Olla'set also maintains that threedees can't possibly be sentient, an opinion that you and I will shortly disprove.

Do you believe there is a higher dimension than our own, Demonai?

I do. Are you willing to accept that there could be? That it could even be inhabited by creatures we are unable to perceive, observing us? Studying us? Perhaps even amusing themselves by creating and playing with us?

Tillah's essence went still. *If that were true, it would be terrifying to contemplate. How can you even think of such things, Demonai?*

Their discussion was interrupted by a sudden high-pitched vibration.

And there is our brand new threedee, said Demonai, feeling as proud as if he had collected and aggregated it himself.

It's so small and feeble.

It will grow larger and stronger over time.

And it isn't sentient, Demonai. Observe its essence. Such a faint and sluggish little light.

That will grow and strengthen over time as well.

How do you know this?

Let me show you.

Their next stop was also a gathering place, but not inside a structure. Demonai and Tillah implanted their pods and observed as a crowd of small and very excited threedees ineffectually pursued a spherical object. Larger threedees, both male and female, were lined up on the borders of the area where this was happening, witnessing the activity and making a great deal of noise.

This is a game, Tillah. There are actually two groups on the field, competing for possession of the sphere.

Then why do they keep repelling it with their pods? Why doesn't one of them just collect it?

Because possession is not the sole end of the game. Each group is working together as a team to accomplish a shared goal, and that is to move the object to a specific location in the opposing team's territory.

Wouldn't this goal be more speedily achieved if the larger threedees became involved?

Yes, but that would defeat the purpose of playing the game. The small threedees are the offspring of the larger ones, and this game is part of their education. You observed how weak the spark is in the essence of a newly-expelled threedee. These creatures have a short life-span, and it takes precious time for their essence to become fully functional. So the larger ones organize activities like this one to exercise the developing essence of their offspring. This way, everything inside the containment membrane reaches its full size and capacity at the same time.

So this game is meant to teach them how to collaborate effectively with other threedees? I imagine that would be a survival skill in a dimension as crowded with matter as this one is, Tillah commented. *However, not all threedees seem to be proficient at it. Observe, Demonai.*

One of the adults had left the sidelines and rushed into the middle of the game, waving his arms as he expressed dissatisfaction with the way it was being played. Tillah and Demonai watched him berate another adult and then take to task one of the smallest threedees, a male offspring who seemed to become even smaller as he was showered with abuse.

That offspring is the threedee we observed being expelled at the hospital.

Poor little creature! Is he making a wish that we could grant?

Tillah's readiness to become actively involved in the threedee world did not escape Demonai's notice. He hoped his gleeful reaction to it escaped hers.

No. He believes that he has failed and deserves to be treated like this, in the presence of other threedees. I know that he survives to full maturity, however. I've already made contact with him later in his life.

Tillah sparkled with amusement. *I'm not surprised. Do I get to meet him too?*

I don't think that would be wise. The knowledge that one being exists in a higher dimension than his own already makes him nervous. If he realizes there is more than one of us....

...he'll be terrified, Tillah supplied, *just as I would be if I thought—never mind. Tell me, Demonai, does he learn in spite of his parent to collaborate effectively with others?*

Too well, I'm afraid. Now he needs to separate himself from the group and achieve things that the others cannot. And I am helping him.

How?

Let me show you.

Their next stop was outdoors as well. Demonai and Tillah implanted themselves together inside a hollow metal container.

We are near the structure where he continues his education, Demonai explained. *Observe.* Carefully, he grasped and lifted an object, reoriented it, then returned the object to a different location.

What did you just do? Tillah wanted to know.

The object I moved is a transportation device. This one belongs to a being who has been creating obstacles to our little friend's success. At his request, I have placed it atop another object, making it difficult for that being to access, so that she will experience the same level of frustration as she has been imposing on others.

Could he not simply communicate his dissatisfaction to her by making sound waves?

He could. But then he would be no different from the many other threedees at this place of learning. Only he is capable of making this particular statement in this particular way.

Because you are helping him?

Yes. I am his sidekick.

CHAPTER EIGHT

2003

March 16, 8:55 a.m.

Boehm blinked, and the woman disappeared.

Okay. This was a dream, he reminded himself. Time could run backwards, things could materialize out of nowhere...

"Darling?" There she was, standing at the foot of the bed, fully dressed, holding a fan made out of credit cards. He loved the symbolism. "I just have to pick up a few things for tomorrow night. Do you mind?"

"Go ahead, knock yourself out," he told her.

Her smile tripled in wattage. "I'll be back in a few hours," she promised, and was gone.

Feeling like Alice about to explore Wonderland, Boehm swung himself out of bed. There were doors in this place, leading to other rooms. What else would he find here? Solid gold bathroom fixtures? A ticker-tape machine in the kitchen? A platoon of yes-men sitting around the dining room table?

His subconscious was having a field day. The bathtub looked like a marble shrine, surrounded by things on pedestals. Boehm glanced at himself in the bathroom mirror – set into the wall, not just attached to it – and found himself staring into the olive-complexioned face of a man he'd often envied, although not for his looks: James A. Hollinger.

The financial guru and media darling had recently turned fifty. He wasn't aging gracefully. There was creasing and puffiness around his eyes. His hair was still mostly dark, with patches of gray at the temples that would have been distinguishing if only Hollinger's forehead weren't so high. In another couple of years he would be flat-out balding. And jowly. And nobody would care. They would still hang on his every word and fall at his feet in adulation, because the man was Filthy Rich.

Hollinger was constantly being interviewed and consulted. If there were a Money Olympics, he would give the color commentary while wannabes competed. No one would dare to fire him from a project—not without some sweetheart handshake that would pay the salaries of a hundred Garrick Boehms for several years.

Boehm opened a cabinet at random. Five shavers sat nestled in rechargers. Not one bore a brand name. Of course. Someone with Hollinger's money could get *everything* custom-made.

Feeling vaguely as though he were committing vandalism, Boehm used the facilities – all of them. Then, with rising anticipation, he went looking for the clothes closet.

It was a walk-in, almost as large as his entire apartment. Thirty suits if there was one. Real silk. Real wool. Tuxedos – plural! A different shirt for each day of the month. At least a dozen pairs of shoes, not counting golf cleats. And the accessories–! For a while, Boehm just stood in the middle of the room and turned a slow circle, devouring all those choices with his eyes. Maybe he wasn't dreaming after all. Maybe he'd died and gone to heaven.

Suddenly, he heard a peremptory knock at one of the doors. Boehm grinned at the face in the mirror and called out, "Come in." Then he snagged a monogrammed bathrobe off its hook and headed for the vestibule, shrugging the garment on as he went.

It was time to meet the next persona in this exceptionally long and vivid dream.

* * * * *

Fortunately, Hollinger had thought to count the money in Claire Amory's purse before getting into the taxi. It wasn't quite enough to get him all the way home from Kew Gardens, but he was damned if he was going to take this body onto a bus or streetcar or – worse – a subway train. So, in exchange for every penny Claire had on her, the cab driver agreed to let him off walking distance away from the condo tower.

Hollinger spent the entire ride rehearsing what he could say to a couple of hysterical women to calm them down. The driver must have thought he was crazy. He probably took a few illegal shortcuts just to get this nut out of his cab.

Nate, the uniformed guard at the entrance to Hollinger's building, was a former pro linebacker. To someone of Claire Amory's stature, he looked like an impassable brick wall. As Hollinger paused, weighing his chances with this fellow, the burly doorman gave him a slow, appraising grin. "You're a new face, Missy. Are you one of Mister Hollinger's private clients?"

James smiled and nodded, unwilling to trust his voice at that moment. Did everyone in the building know about his annual 'vacation'?

"Well, your timing's perfect. Here, let me get that inside door for you." To Hollinger's combined astonishment and dismay, Nate not only let a perfect stranger into the building, he even tipped his hat to her.

"Thank you," said James, smiling his most charming smile while making a mental note to fire the doorman the moment he was back in his own body.

All the way up in the elevator, he steeled himself to walk in on a scene of chaos – two distraught women, one in a man's body, hurling insults and various breakable objects at each other. Not until he was actually standing at the entrance to the penthouse did the chilling thought occur to him: How would Claire Amory react when she saw her own body walk through the door?

Hollinger paused, one fist poised to knock, as his stomach

sank in sudden dread. Maybe it had been a mistake to come here alone in such a short, slight body. Maybe he should have brought someone with him. Someone like Nate.

All at once, Hollinger heard male laughter. It was faint, but definitely coming from the other side of the door. His door. And *his apartment*, he reminded himself sternly.

He knocked.

"Come in," sang out a very familiar-sounding voice.

Hollinger tried the knob and felt his stomach sink a second time. The door was unlocked. He nudged it open and peered cautiously around it before entering the suite.

The vestibule was in perfect order. So was the living room. Now he was confused. What the hell was going on here?

Just then, his body strode in and sat down at one end of the gold and gray divan. Hollinger watched in fascination as it crossed its legs, arranged the folds of its dressing gown -- *his* dressing gown, he thought savagely -- and beamed expectantly at the new arrival. Ms Amory was obviously feeling relaxed and well-rested and – well – *satisfied*.

Hollinger smiled with his lips and asked through gritted teeth, "Where is Roxanne?"

"The blonde? Is that her name? Lovely woman. She said she had to pick up a few things."

Of course. Nate had told him his timing was perfect. One woman leaves, and the next one arrives. "How many cards?" he sighed.

"Cards?"

"Credit cards, you—! How many did she take with her?"

"Four or five, I guess. I didn't count them."

Hollinger cursed under his breath. Every year Roxanne went out to 'pick up a few things'. Every year she asked to take one of his platinum cards with her and he put a thousand dollars in cash into her hand instead. He didn't mind letting her shop with his money, but there had to be limits. If Roxanne maxed out even one of those cards, this would be the most expensive 'vacation' James Hollinger had ever had.

Carefully, he placed Claire Amory's faux leather handbag on the ebony console table beside a silver tray holding a leaded crystal decanter and several sherry glasses. Then, just as carefully, he composed his features and said, "You're probably wondering what is going on."

"Not really. This is pretty straightforward, as dreams go. The symbolism is very transparent."

No wonder she was sitting there so relaxed. Well, it was time to stress her out a little. "Listen, Claire—"

"Who's Claire?"

"You are, sweetie."

She shrugged. "If you say so. I've actually never thought of myself as that type, but I guess I can appreciate a metaphor as well as the next person. So if I'm a man with a woman's name, you must be a woman with a man's name. What is it? George? Albert?"

She was infuriating. "Stop trying to turn this into some kind of party game," he snapped. "I'm James Hollinger, and you are in my body."

Still grinning idiotically, the body in the dressing gown nodded its head. "This is wonderful," she said admiringly. "I hope I can remember all of it and write it down when I wake up."

"When you wake up?" he almost shouted. "You *are* awake, dammit!"

For the first time, the friendly smile faltered. "That's impossible," said the woman in Hollinger's body with maddening calm. "None of this is real."

"None of this?" He was stupefied. "What about Roxanne?"

"A metaphor. Like you, like this apartment. It's all symbolic of my innermost emotions and wishes. I always wanted to live a millionaire's life, and in this lucid dream, I'm finally getting my chance. I don't know whose body you have there, but you obviously represent something very negative about my subconscious, and I want you to leave now."

Feeling his gorge rising, Hollinger took a shuddering breath. "Now, see here, Miss Amory, or Ms Amory, or whatever you want to call yourself –"

"I'd rather not call myself either one."

"I'm sure you wouldn't, you goddamned pervert! You can deny it all you like, but this is your body that I'm trapped inside. You are Claire Amory. I am James A. Hollinger. Somehow, our minds were switched during the night. And no, doll-face, you are *not* dreaming, and neither am I, though I wish to hell I were."

The other person's face fell. "Oh, dear."

"That's putting it mildly."

"No, you don't understand. I'm not Claire Amory. I'm Garry Boehm. I'm a man."

Suddenly, Hollinger felt the nausea returning. "You're a man?" he echoed weakly.

Boehm nodded.

"Then where is Claire Amory's mind? And where is your body?"

"Probably together. We're a triangle. How exciting! The symbolism in this dream just keeps getting more and more complex."

The pounding in Hollinger's temples signaled a definite rise in blood pressure. "How many times do I have to tell you that this is not—!" He paused for a steadying breath, then continued in a more controlled voice, "We have to find them, Garry. Your body and her mind. This is serious."

"Why not just wait here?" came the infuriatingly serene reply. "My body, my dream. Anything's possible."

"You moron! What do I have to do to convince you that you're awake?"

Hollinger tried to recall the old tales he'd heard about dreams. A person who dreamed about falling would awaken before hitting bottom. No good – the penthouse was on the twelfth floor, and in any case, he wanted his body back in good condition. Should he have this Boehm fellow pack a suitcase? Not good either – if he finished packing and actually closed the valise he would think he was dead.

"Slap my face," Boehm suggested quietly.

"What?"

"I've never had much tolerance for pain," he explained with a shrug, "and any time I've dreamt about being physically attacked I've always awakened at once. Slap me."

He'd been itching to do it anyway. Obediently, Hollinger delivered an openhanded blow that left his palm stinging. Boehm slowly raised a hand to cradle his bruised cheek as his jaw dropped in utter amazement.

"Good Lord," he breathed, "you're real." He gazed wonderingly around the living room, not one detail of which had changed. "This place is real. And Roxanne?"

"Roxanne was real," James confirmed with a sigh. *Not to mention bloody expensive.*

"I've been deflowered," Boehm murmured in disbelief. Then his eyes rolled upward as he toppled sideways on the divan.

* * * * *

Claire's destination was a rooming house in the Beaches, a neighborhood of older houses in the east end of the city close to the lakeshore. This building in particular was a sprawl of red bricks badly in need of new pointing and joined to the sidewalk by several worn and pitted concrete steps. The dark green front door was peeling, and the dozen or so windows that faced the street hadn't been thoroughly cleaned in years. Nonetheless, it was the promise of what she expected to find inside that set her to humming as she bounded up the front steps and through the door.

Claire then took the three flights of stairs two at a time, pausing outside her room just long enough for several deep, calming breaths. She didn't want to come on too strong. For a man, simply waking up in a woman's body would have been traumatic. Any sudden loud noise on top of that could send him right over the edge.

Gently, carefully, she rapped on the door.

There was no answer.

Licking her lips nervously, she tapped a little harder. Still no response.

When a third, more aggressive knock failed to rouse anybody inside, Claire tried the knob. The room was locked.

There was only one thing left to do. Glancing around furtively, she reached into her pants pocket and took out the wallet containing Garrick Boehm's identification. Unfortunately, Boehm didn't have a credit card she could ruin. His library card was plastic, though.

It worked. Silently the door swung open on a room that looked as though a cyclone had torn through it. Drawers had been yanked open and their contents spilled onto the bed and the floor. Her underwear had been all but tied in knots by what had apparently been a frantic search for valuables. Claire's heart dropped. Her laptop and printer were still on the bridge table where she'd left them last night; but she'd been robbed of something far more precious than that. Her body was gone, and she had no idea where.

It had, however, left something sour-smelling behind in the plastic bag lining her waste basket. As Claire tied the bag closed for the trash bin, she considered a depressing list of possibilities.

If he'd run outside screaming, wearing only a nightgown, he could be in a psychiatric ward right now; on the other hand, if he'd retained sufficient presence of mind to get dressed, he could have taken refuge with a relative (who might or might not have the same last name as his), or with a good friend, in which case all she could do was—

A sudden knocking derailed Claire's train of thought, as Mrs. Scotti, the landlady, called through the door, "*Bella*, I'm going to the store. Is there anything you need?"

Without thinking, Claire replied, "No, thanks," then gasped as she realized what she had done. She'd answered in a masculine voice. Mrs. Scotti was the busiest busybody in the whole neighborhood; and if she had heard Garrick Boehm screaming in Claire's voice earlier...

"What?" shouted Mrs. Scotti. "Claire, are you in there? Are you all right? Answer me!"

Claire groaned inwardly. There was no way she could reply. Even her silence was an indictment.

"Listen, you!" Mrs. Scotti's voice was painfully shrill. "I'm calling the police!"

Of course. And they'd have no problem at all believing that there was a body missing. The missing mind, on the other hand – that would be a much tougher sell. A peculiar whirlpool sensation had begun in the pit of Claire's stomach. She had to get away, preferably without letting Mrs. Scotti get a good look at her new face. The window was her only option. Out onto the fire escape and down to the alley.

Her plan would have worked much better if Claire had been wearing her own body. Boehm's knees got caught in the window-frame. Then his size twelves refused to clear the sill. Once outside they got stuck in the wrought-iron railing, nearly pitching her head-first down the slippery stairs to the pavement below.

Aching all over – again – she finally limped out onto Queen Street, rubbing at several bruises on her left arm. When this ordeal was done, she decided grimly, somebody was going to pay for it.

For a long while Claire walked, not sure where she might go, feeling only that for some reason it refused to divulge, the universe had decided to gang up on her. Who was this Garrick Boehm, anyway, and why didn't he have a driver's licence? You didn't have to own a car to have a driver's licence. Claire had a driver's licence, had even renewed it the previous year, and she hadn't driven anything since leaving Caverley Corners. How could he not be carrying his home address on him?

Suddenly, she looked up and found herself staring at the facade of Sophie Hopper's apartment building. Claire's spirits leaped.

Sophie had always been supportive, hadn't she? And perceptive. Sophie was extremely perceptive. If anyone could look beyond this rumpled white lab coat and recognize a friend in need of comforting, it would be Sophie Hopper, Claire was certain. And even if she didn't recognize Claire at first, she would still offer her help. She had to. Sophie was a nurse at Toronto Mercy Hospital.

Claire glanced at the digital watch on her new body's wrist and did some swift mental calculation. Sophie's duty shift began at noon. She might still be at home. Even if she weren't, the ride up to her apartment and back would be warming, at least. It was a little chilly to be strolling outside without a jacket.

Her timing was perfect. Sophie was on her way out, locking her apartment door behind her just as Claire stepped off the elevator on the third floor.

She was an impressive sight, was Sophie Hopper – five-foot-ten in flat shoes and so delightfully curved that not even the shapeless all-weather coat she wore could disguise her figure. Her perfect oval face was surrounded by a mass of flaming red hair, thick enough that it appeared to be exploding upward from her shoulders. Claire waited for her to turn around before calling out, "Sophie! Am I glad to see you!"

Taken by surprise, Sophie frowned at the disheveled stranger for several seconds. "I don't know you," she said in a hard, flat voice. "Get away from me, you creep."

Claire's heart sank. Part of her wanted to skulk away and hide. But the rest of her wouldn't let it.

"Sophie, please! You've got to help me. I'm not the person you think you see," she cried.

Unmoved, Sophie glared at this personage who dared block her way to the elevator and snapped, "Listen, buster, you may think a nurse is an easy mark, but things have changed. I don't know how you know my name, but you'd better forget it fast and get the hell out of my way or I'll deck you."

Common sense should have taken over at that moment. Claire should have remembered that self-defence was a compulsory subject at the Florence Nightingale School of Nursing Science, where Sophie had obtained her degree. It should have occurred to Claire that a woman nearly six feet tall who worked out four times a week and had a green belt in judo was probably a match for any man who accosted her under any circumstances. But it didn't.

"You're going to hear me out," Claire declared recklessly. "Let's go inside and talk." Then she grabbed Sophie by the arm.

There was no warning. "Ee-*yah!*" screamed the redhead, and suddenly Claire felt herself flying through the air. She landed with a painful thud, slid several feet across the terrazzo floor and fetched up against the closed elevator door.

"Now will you leave me alone?" Sophie demanded.

Claire struggled to clear her head and collect the sprawling parts of Boehm's rangy body. "No, dammit," she muttered. "You do know me and I can prove it." Slowly she got to her feet. "Last

October you went out with a guy named Al Poteski, as a favor to a friend. He had too much to drink and tried to force his attentions on you and you broke his arm. Now, who's the person you called for help that evening, to get him to the hospital and back up your story about an accidental fall?"

To Claire's amazement, Sophie's expression became even colder and harder. "Oh, so that's your game, is it?" she snarled. "Blackmail? Ee-*yah!*"

This time Claire finished in a crumpled heap at the feet of a gray-haired woman in a blue cardigan and a blue-and-white printed housedress. Focusing with great difficulty, Claire watched the elevator door open to admit Sophie Hopper. There was a long pause before it closed again. Perhaps there was still time to—

"Get him, Mrs. Griesdorf!" Sophie called out stridently.

Then something hard hit Claire on the head and all the lights went out in her brain.

* * * * *

After some discussion, they had decided to leave Hollinger's cars parked in the garage beneath his building and take a taxi to Boehm's place, where his body would eventually have to turn up.

Boehm lived in a one-bedroom apartment in a section of the city that was ripe for urban renewal. The building superintendent was a little ripe too, Hollinger couldn't help noticing as he watched Boehm count bills into the man's already-greasy palm. Finally, the door was unlocked and the two changelings stepped inside.

"So, what do you think?" Boehm asked. "It isn't the penthouse, but…"

"… it's home," Hollinger finished for him. "It's okay." Actually, he thought, it was better than okay. It was definitely more spacious than the room in which he'd awakened that morning, and it was clean and comfortable as well, even though most of the furniture looked as though it had come from a thrift store. He glanced around, nodded slowly, and added, "Reminds me a little of my first place."

Boehm uttered a derisive snort of laughter. "Really? Which part? The exclusive location, or the elegant décor?"

Hollinger decided he'd had enough. "You want to put a lid on the sarcasm? I didn't inherit what you saw back in the penthouse, Garry. I worked bloody hard to get it, starting at the bottom. Hard work creates opportunities, and courage takes advantage of them. So if you don't happen to like the shape of your life so far, you'd better look elsewhere for a target, because I'm damned if you're going to take out your money-envy on me!"

As though blown over by Hollinger's burst of anger, Boehm sagged into the overstuffed armchair near the window and ran a weary hand over his face. "I'm sorry," he sighed. "You're right. It's just that I lost my job yesterday because of money. Some muckety-muck in the government canceled my funding."

"So, you find another job. Or you invent something and start your own company. What's the big deal?"

"Well, for starters," Boehm reminded him, "I first have to get back into my own body. Or maybe I'd rather not. Maybe I'd prefer to remain James Hollinger and enjoy life as a multimillionaire."

Hollinger laughed. "Wealth and fame, eh? You think that's all it's about? I guarantee, you'd soon discover what a headache my life can be. Speaking of which," he added, "how much did you have to bribe the super to let us in?"

Boehm blushed. "A hundred dollars."

"What?"

"I offered him twenty but he recognized your face and demanded more," Boehm explained uncomfortably. "And then I had to sweeten the bribe so he'd be quiet and not alert the media."

"You see? It starts already."

* * * * *

For the second time that day, Claire awakened in a room she didn't recall entering.

In the semi-darkness, some sort of being was silhouetted against what appeared to be a distant wall. The being came slowly toward her and then bent over her, its wheezing breath hot against her face, the one luminous eye in the middle of its head glowing yellow. Closer and closer the pupilless eye came...

Paralyzed by fear, Claire wanted to scream. But her ribs ached so much that it was all she could do just to keep breathing. Meanwhile the being's eye was moving from one side of its head to the other. It moved away, then leaned even closer over her.

All at once there was pressure on both sides of her head. And at that moment, something inside Claire snapped. "Aaugh!" she yelled, and flailed both her arms.

"Ow! Dammit!" said the being.

The lights came on. A dark-haired man in a white jacket was standing near the door with a hand clapped over his right eye. Tears were streaming from his left eye. As he stepped away from the wall, the door to the little room flew open; its edge slammed hard into his left shoulder, and he gasped and stopped in his tracks, a long-suffering expression stamped on his features.

The nurse who had opened the door, a tall dark-skinned girl in a two-piece uniform, was immediately contrite. "Are you all right, doctor?" she inquired.

"I'll let you know," he replied through gritted teeth.

"Isn't that your ophthalmoscope on the floor?"

"Yes," he grated. "I want you to go back to the desk and get me a discharge form for this patient."

"But, doctor—"

"Now, nurse, while I still have the use of my writing hand!"

With an anxious look at Claire, the nurse scurried out the door. The doctor closed it after her rather forcefully and then limped to the side of the examining table.

"Welcome back, Doctor Boehm. You're in a hospital," he said, his face wearing a caricature of a smile and his soft, strangely husky voice casting a menacing pall over every reassuring word that came out of his mouth. "There's no need to be frightened. I'm Doctor Forsythe. We've been taking good care of you here. You've had a bump on the head, but it looks as though you're going to be all right. And because we'd like to keep it that way, I've decided to send you home to recuperate."

"But I've been unconscious. Shouldn't there be tests, an MRI, an X-ray at least?"

"Already done," he snapped. "We found no fracture, and the hematoma is outside the skull. You're good to go."

"I'm sorry about your ophthalmoscope. I didn't mean to break it."

"I know," he reassured her, still wearing that pasted-on smile. "None of it was deliberate. Your gurney rolling over my foot, the muscle spasm that rammed your hand into my throat, the damaged capillaries around my eye, which are no doubt hemorrhaging as we speak...." He paused and heaved a regretful sigh. "We had an excellent employee safety record here until you arrived, Boehm. Please, do us all a favor and go home." And he left, slamming the door behind him.

Claire wanted to cry. She had a headache. She probably had a concussion. How could any doctor send a patient home in her condition without a period of observation?

Just then the door to the examining room flew open again. "Here he is," said Forsythe's voice. Suddenly the room was full of dark blue uniform as two large police officers stepped inside, followed by the injured physician. Now what?

"Are you preferring charges?" Claire stammered, panic rising in her chest.

"No," Forsythe replied, "and neither are the two women you

attacked. Lucky you. These gentlemen are going to escort you home."

And judging by the grimness of their expressions, they'd probably been ordered to shoot her if she tried to escape.

* * * * *

Boehm and Hollinger made a lunch out of what was on hand and then devoured it hungrily -- tomato soup, hot dogs and macaroni and cheese. Hollinger waited for some kind of snide comment from his host – 'Sorry, we seem to be out of filet mignon.' – but Boehm carefully refrained. Good. Their immediate problem was far too serious for either of them to be wasting time or energy sniping at the other. Besides, Hollinger was experiencing food with Claire Amory's taste buds, and they *liked* macaroni and cheese.

The furniture in Boehm's apartment, it turned out, had been rented because the scientist couldn't afford to buy his own. But the dishes and pots and pans were his. Hollinger couldn't help noticing that they were well cared-for and of fine quality.

When the two changelings had finished eating, Boehm insisted on washing up right away. Half an hour later they were sitting side by side on the sofa, reading National Geographic magazines and waiting for Boehm's body to come home.

They didn't have long to wait. Shortly before two o'clock they heard the sound of feet ascending the stairs to the second floor. And voices. Three of them. Catching their breath simultaneously, the two men listened hard as the feet stopped in front of Boehm's apartment door and an interminable *click-scratch-click* began of keys being tried in the lock.

Hollinger motioned silently to Boehm to move to the wall behind the door. They got there just in time. With a gentle creak, the door swung partway open.

"All right, sir," came a man's voice from the hallway, "we'll leave you now. With that kind of injury, you'll be disoriented for a while, so it would be best to stay at home. And remember what the doctor said – the one you didn't hurt. If you begin to feel dizzy or sick to your stomach, or if your eyesight goes wonky, call for an ambulance. Just make sure you tell them to take you anywhere but Toronto Mercy Hospital. Okay?"

"I'll be fine, officer, just fine," was the faint reply.

"You're lucky we were able to talk those two women out of pressing charges," a third voice advised. "Now you just take it easy for a while. And the next time you get an urge to accost someone in a public place, do yourself a favor and walk away."

"I will. Thanks."

As two pairs of feet set off down the stairs, Boehm's body dragged itself wearily inside the apartment. The second the door closed, Boehm and Hollinger pounced. Hollinger seized the left arm, Boehm the right. Too overwhelmed to put up a struggle, Claire let herself be half-pulled and half-carried to the sofa, where they sat her down with a fat *thud!* before moving in from both sides at once.

"Are you hurt? Where? How did it happen?" Boehm demanded, as Hollinger, sitting on her other side, yelled, "Charges? What charges?"

Claire's gaze swung helplessly from one scowling face to the other. One of them was her own, barely recognizable behind the angry expression it was wearing. Just the sight of it made her feel light-headed. So she did the only thing she could under the circumstances – she burst into tears.

"This has been the worst day of my entire life," she blubbered.

Boehm couldn't stand to watch himself cry. He got up and began pacing the living room as Hollinger reached up and put a consoling arm around the broad shoulders shuddering beside him on the sofa.

"Claire?" he ventured when it appeared the storm was letting up.

"Yes," she replied between sniffles. "Are you Garrick Boehm?"

"No, he is," said Hollinger, pointing to the long-legged body pacing the floor impatiently in front of them.

Her face alight with sudden comprehension, Claire gasped and exclaimed, "You mean there were three of us switched around?"

"I'm afraid so. I'm James A. Hollinger."

"I know. I recognized your—" She cleared her throat and started over. "So, we have a financial wizard, an author, and a…" She glanced down at the smudged and wrinkled lab coat she was wearing.

"… particle physicist," Boehm supplied, rising impatience putting an edge on his voice. Abruptly, he stopped pacing and dropped into the armchair opposite the other two changelings. "Now that the introductions are over, and before I bring out the tea and crumpets, would you please explain how you managed to make my body *persona non grata* at a major hospital?"

Hollinger shook his head. "I think it's more important that she tell us how she ended up in hospital in the first place, Garry."

They both turned and stared at her expectantly. In that moment, Claire realized how bizarre her story was going to sound. She was having her adventure, all right, but who in their right mind would believe it?

"It's a bad joke," she warned them.

"Go ahead," said Hollinger. "We could use a laugh."

She told them everything that had happened to her that day.

"Wait a minute," said Boehm. "You actually thought that this woman would be able to recognize you, even though you'd been transformed into a man?"

She shrugged. "Pretty naive, huh?"

"I'd call it idealistic," Hollinger corrected her. "That sort of stuff happens in the movies, Claire. In real life, unfortunately, most people judge solely by appearances."

"But we're best friends. At least, we were," she sighed. "Once you've wiped the floor with somebody, I imagine it's hard to get back to the original relationship."

Boehm leaned forward in his chair. "Green belt in judo, you said?"

She nodded. "And a loaded handbag, swung with force. I probably have a concussion."

"You're probably lucky to be alive," Boehm declared. "And they were thinking of charging *you* with assault?"

"I sure wish I knew what was going on," said Claire wistfully.

"Well, one thing we do know," Hollinger told her. "There were only three of us involved and we're all here. Now we need to plan."

Boehm groaned. "Now, *that's* naive. Plan what? Until we know *how* we were switched around…"

"… we somehow have to deal with day-to-day obligations. Claire, what do you do for a living again?"

"I'm a writer. Why?"

"Freelance?"

She nodded.

"Perfect! You work out of a home office, I'm on vacation, and Garry's unemployed. So we can all stay here and take as long as necessary to figure a way out of our predicament."

"Whoa!" said Boehm. "Why here? Why not at the huge and comfy penthouse?"

Hollinger paused for effect. "Roxanne."

"She's a beautiful woman. What's your point?"

"Remember what we had to pay the super to be quiet about us? Roxanne wouldn't settle for cash. She would insist on a wedding ring."

"Worth millions and determined to marry for love. Now, *that's* idealistic," Claire remarked with a smile.

"She went shopping with a fistful of your credit cards," Boehm reminded him. "Shouldn't your body be there to retrieve them when she comes back?"

"That loose end is already taken care of," Hollinger declared. "I made a phone call from the penthouse before we left."

"If Roxanne is taken care of, then what's the problem with camping out at your place for the duration?" Boehm persisted.

"It's not just Roxanne," Hollinger sighed. "It's Nate, the doorman, not to mention the news media – the paparazzi are always watching my place. Sometimes I think my phone is bugged as well. Here, at least, we've got some privacy."

"Think again. Here, we've got Rosseau, the building superintendent," Boehm pointed out sharply. "Or is paying off blackmailers just a routine expense for you?"

Hollinger stared at him sadly and replied, "When you're James A. Hollinger, my friend, nothing comes free of charge, including and especially privacy."

CHAPTER NINE

Everything was happening exactly as Demonai had predicted it would.

You're wrong. They're running around in mindless confusion, declared Tillah.

Confusion, yes, but not mindless. Their actions are purposeful. All three of them realized immediately that before they could begin addressing the unanswered questions regarding their current situation, they needed to gather in one location. This indicates intelligence.

Confused intelligence. They lack information, Demonai, and with their limited perceptual abilities they aren't likely to come across it any time soon.

You need to give them more credit. Threedees are natural problem-solvers, drawn to discrepancies and unanswered questions. That's the first thing I noticed about them. They're quite resourceful, and it's precisely to observe how they resolve the mystery of a predicament like this one that I'm running the experiment.

Really? I thought you just wanted to see how they would react to being toyed with.

Originally, yes. But the experiment has evolved. The more I learn about these creatures, the more I want to find out about them.

That in itself is very interesting, Demonai, because I have observed that the more you find out about them, the more like them you seem to become. This may be a negative consequence of being compacted and confined for so long in five dimensions. I'm trying to decide whether to ask Olla'set to release you as an act of mercy.

No, Tillah, I don't need to be rescued. What I need is for Olla'set to join me here so he can learn about the threedees. Surely he must be curious about what I'm doing inside this bubble.

Actually, he isn't. After each visit with you, I meld with him and share information. He knows everything that you and I have observed about these creatures.

He may know what we have observed, but he doesn't know what we know about them.

And what do we know, Demonai? That they are born small and weak but grow and develop into adults. That the adults teach their offspring how to be members of a society. That they communicate with one another by generating sound waves. That the strong threedees tend to abuse the weak. I'm sorry, Demonai, but we know nothing about them that would convince Olla'set to change his mind about their sentience, or even to come and take a closer look at them.

Then let me show you something that might.

Demonai had been saving this, hoping he wouldn't have to use it. He guided Tillah to the final stop on the tour.

What is this gathering place? It's certainly full of objects. There is hardly room for the threedees to move around inside it.

Some of the threedees choose to spend their lives trying to understand the universe. They have an overwhelming desire to acquire knowledge about the nature of reality, and they do much of their investigating in places like this.

Aren't we going to implant our pods?

No. You are going to meld with one of the threedees, and see what she is seeing at this moment.

Gently, carefully, Demonai coaxed a pod of the threedee's essence into fifth dimensional space and showed Tillah how to connect with it.

At once, Tillah's essence began to spark. *Demonai! She sees a living creature, one that is as differently made from the threedees as they are from us. How is this possible?*

The third dimension is filled with life, Tillah, both sentient and nonsentient, from extremely large to extremely small, made in many different ways. The beings we have been studying are aware of all the other creatures that surround them and thirst to know more about them. So they have invented this device to assist with their observations by making the tiniest life forms appear much larger. What do you observe about the creature under the microscope?

Its shape keeps changing. Its essence is quite visible and it appears to be contained in a flexible membrane... Tillah's essence went still again. *It's made the same way we are. Is it sentient, Demonai?*

It might be. You are melded with the threedee who is studying it. What does she believe?

Tillah paused to sample the threedee's thoughts before replying, *She considers it to be an extremely primitive form of life. She has no plans to attempt to communicate with it. Demonai, is that how our kind would look to a higher-order being? Just a sac full of essence, drifting through its corner of the universe, ingesting whatever matter it comes across, occasionally reproducing by breaking in two?*

I'm sorry I had to upset you by showing you this, Tillah, but it's important that you understand why I keep insisting that Olla'set join us inside the bubble. Reality is much more than our aggregator thinks it is.

So there is a higher dimension than ours?

I'm afraid so.

With sentient beings in it, observing us?

Yes.

How can you be certain, Demonai?

How do you think I was able to remove this bubble from Olla'set's collection sac without his knowledge? How do you think I even knew I ought to?

You have a sidekick!

Tillah, the threedees consider the tiny creature under the microscope to be nonsentient because its life is limited to a small number of activities carried out in specific and unvarying ways, and it never tries to be more or better than it already is. Tell Olla'set that he fits that same definition, and unless he is willing to join me, to learn and grow and become receptive to ideas that contradict his own beliefs, his very existence might be in danger.

CHAPTER TEN

1970

October 1, 4:00 p.m.

Mac returned to the apartment in a jubilant mood and went straight to the fridge to get a beer. Slattery hadn't moved from the sofa. He also hadn't progressed very far in the novel he was reading.

"You've outdone yourself this time, man," declared Mac, clapping a congratulatory hand on Rick's shoulder before dropping into the easy chair beside him. He took a swallow of his beer and continued, "The whole campus is buzzing right now. Rothstein nearly had a heart attack when he saw his office door. You should have been there. His face went from white to beet red. He called out the campus police *and* the fire department, and ordered them to use their axes to chop him a grown-up-sized entrance. It's going to take a week to install a new doorway and clean up the mess. Rick, come on, man, I realize that a magician hates to reveal his secrets, but…"

"… you're dying to know how I did it? I told you before, man."

Still holding his beer, Mac uttered an exasperated syllable and flopped back against his chair, letting his head loll backwards. "The genie?" he complained to the ceiling. "Okay. Fine. Be like that. But I have to warn you, that one's getting old, my friend."

Rick said nothing, just sighed and closed his book.

Mac sat up straight again, his eyes sparkling with mischief. "You know Eddie, the first year student who helps out in the registrar's office sometimes? He was at the pub this afternoon, and he says there's talk about bringing a team of researchers up here to investigate the paranormal activity on campus. Paranormal activity – that's you, bro. What do you think? Should we cook up something special for them, send them home convinced the campus is haunted?"

Suddenly Mac noticed how quiet and thoughtful Slattery had become, and his broad grin faded. "We missed you today, man. Are you feeling okay?"

"Yeah. I just had some thinking to do. There won't be any more pranks, Mac. Rothstein's door was my last gig. We're in our final year and I need to concentrate on graduating from this place."

"Just like that? You're going to quit?"

"I am. I've thought about it, and it's the best way for all concerned."

Mac studied him for a moment, then leaned forward, the corners of his mouth quirking. "Your tank is empty, isn't it? You really did outdo yourself yesterday, and you're afraid there's no way you can top it."

"I guess that's as good a rationale as any. The end result is going to be the same."

Struck by a sudden thought, Mac began to chuckle.

"What?"

"I'm just imagining you giving a genie his pink slip."

They both fell silent again, feeling the weight of Slattery's decision hang over the room.

"Wow," Mac murmured at last. "The legendary prankster is retiring. This is huge, Rick. I feel like I'm witnessing the end of an era."

"It's the end of something, that's for sure."

CHAPTER ELEVEN

2003

Still March 16, 4:05 p.m.

Swallowing his trepidations, Hollinger climbed the steps and walked through the front door of the weary little building that had been Claire's address until that morning. He felt like an impostor about to be revealed by some subtle flaw in his disguise: the wrong tone of his voice, a giveaway gesture of hands or head, a sudden, inexplicable memory lapse totally unlike the woman he was impersonating. Perspiring freely, he paused at the foot of the stairs, beside a door marked A-1.

Suddenly the door was flung open by a dumpy little woman who obviously hadn't been expecting to find anyone standing in front of it. She shrieked and jumped back a step.

"Claire!" she scolded. "Don't do that. You just took ten years off my life."

"Sorry about that," Hollinger muttered.

"Actually, I'm glad you're back," the woman continued chattily. "Let me walk you upstairs to your room. I'm afraid you're in for a shock."

"Oh?"

"A man broke in this morning, left your place a real mess. "

It was all Hollinger could do just to keep a straight face.

"I called the police, of course," she went on, "but by the time they got here he was gone."

He had Claire's key in his hand, but the woman whipped out a passkey and fitted it in the lock before he could make a move. "I never saw him, but I'm sure I would recognize that voice if I ever heard it again."

"Well, uh, thank you for telling me," Hollinger stammered uneasily. But the landlady stood in the doorway, watching him, like a bellhop waiting for a tip.

"Aren't you going to check that nothing is missing?" she finally asked.

The room was exactly as he had left it that morning, but Hollinger went through the motions of searching, since that was clearly the only way to get rid of this prepossessing busybody. When he had turned the place upside-down – again – and could tell her convincingly that nothing had been stolen, the landlady nodded grimly and left.

Alone at last, he thought, pulling Claire's suitcase down from the overhead shelf in the closet.

It had been decided that since he and Claire would both be moving in with Boehm for the duration, they ought to have their personal possessions with them. Accordingly, two lists had been drawn up and the appropriate bodies had been dispatched to fetch the 'necessities of life'.

Claire's list was short: some clothing, her toiletries, and her laptop. She had begun writing a story and she intended to finish it. Hollinger set about removing the specified items from drawers, closet and bathroom, adding the occasional extra that caught his fancy. After all, he reasoned, since he was the one who was going to be wearing all this stuff there should be something about it that he personally liked, such as the pale gray silk scarf, and the brown doeskin gloves he'd found scrunched at the back of a drawer. As for the toiletries, after stealing a whiff of Claire's favorite perfume he decided he'd rather smell of soap.

Finally, following her written instructions, he put the laptop into its shoulder-strapped carrying case along with the other items she'd listed, all found on the folding card table: the charger and cables, a mouse, a flash drive, some hand-written notes and a half-empty package of brown manila envelopes.

As he was zipping all the laptop case's pockets closed, there was a sudden knock at the door. Hollinger froze, then forced himself to relax. After all, people judged by appearances. Anyone not aware of the situation would look at him and see Claire Amory. The worst thing he could do right now, he told himself sternly, was behave like an intruder.

Warily, Hollinger went to the door and opened it...and nearly crumpled under the weight of the tall, red-haired woman who immediately fell into his arms, moaning, "Oh, Claire!"

Good Lord, what now?

"Come on in," he offered faintly.

The amazon gazed deeply into his widened eyes and said huskily, "I knew I could count on you, Claire."

She was obviously very upset. Before he'd even closed the door she was pacing rapidly back and forth.

"You wouldn't believe how agitated I've been all day," she declared. "I thrashed around the charge desk for a while until Pat finally sent me home to grind my axe where I wouldn't disturb the patients."

Suddenly Hollinger realized that she was wearing a white uniform under her all-weather coat. "Why don't you sit down?" he suggested nervously.

"Oh, I couldn't," she declared, plopping herself down on the edge of the bed. "I'm much too tense to relax. Claire, I was attacked by a man this morning as I left my apartment. He looked as though he'd slept in his clothes and smelled as though he hadn't changed them in a week. And he had wild eyes – a crazy man's eyes. And he was wearing a white lab coat. Oh, God, maybe he was an escapee from a mental institution."

Or maybe he was a she...?

"But what really gets me," the amazon went on excitedly, "is that he knew my name and where I lived. Now I'm afraid to go home."

"You've got a green belt in judo and you're afraid to go home?" he repeated incredulously.

The woman exhaled an impatient syllable. "Listen, the judo makes me hard to attack. It can't make me indestructible. And what if he's waiting for me with a knife this time? Or a gun?"

For the first time since the redhead had entered the room, Hollinger relaxed. So this distraught young lady was the formidable Sophie?

"Claire, I hate to ask this of you," Sophie began, wringing her hands into a prayerful knot. "I know there's barely room enough for one adult in this place, but would it be all right if I spent the night here? I could sleep on the floor, and –" Suddenly she noticed the suitcase standing beside the door. "Are you going away?"

He shrugged. "For a while."

"I don't blame you. I always wondered how anyone could be creative in surroundings like this," Sophie said with a slight shudder. "But where are you go—" She gasped softly. "Oh, honey, I hope you weren't planning to crash at my place. As long as that maniac is on the loose, you're much safer somewhere else."

Hollinger's thoughts began to pick up speed. "Actually, I have this friend. I'm minding his apartment. And that gives me an idea. Why don't you move in here for a few days? If you think you can stand the décor for that long."

Her face brightened at once. "Are you sure? I still have the spare key you gave me for emergencies, but I would never just—"

"Of course I'm sure," he replied. "I'll call and let you know when I'm coming back so you can—"

"Oh, Claire, you're one in a million!"

Sophie leaped up and threw her arms around him. Caught off-guard, he had to struggle not to panic. It was, after all, a gesture of affection. Hollinger counted slowly to three before attempting to disengage himself from her powerful embrace.

"Well," he said shakily, "I'd better be off."

"But you'll still be coming to the meeting tonight, won't you?"

Alarms began going off in Hollinger's head. Meeting? Claire hadn't mentioned any meeting.

"Oh – sure," he stammered. "The usual place?"

"Right. Only don't forget that we're starting fifteen minutes earlier than normal."

"I'll be there," he assured her with a weak smile. Hollinger could almost feel his disguise flaking off. Any second now, his sideburns would pop out. "Bye now." And, with the amazon's eyes following him like targeting lasers, he floated Claire's belongings out the door on a sea of nervous perspiration.

* * * * *

As Boehm was folding shirts in the powder-blue bedroom of the penthouse, he heard the telephone ring. Three rings later, he was still staring at the cordless receiver in its cradle on the night stand and dithering over whether to pick up. Then the answering machine cut in: "Hello, this is James A. Hollinger. Please leave a message at the tone and I'll try to get back to you as soon as possible."

"Don't bother, you scumbag creep!"

Boehm froze. The voice was harsh, even abrasive, but it belonged unmistakably to Roxanne. "How dare you! How *dare* you cancel your credit cards right after sending me out to shop with them? You bastard! And I'd just found the perfect dress to wear as your date to that cocktail party tomorrow night. The police told me I must have misunderstood your instructions. I suppose I should be grateful you didn't tell them I stole the damned things.

So what happened, you son of a bitch? Did you finally have second thoughts about taking a commoner like me to such an important do? Couldn't find the balls to tell me that to my face? Just like you haven't got the balls to pick up the phone and talk to me right now? Well, Jimmy, we're through. You hear me? I never want to see you or hear from you again."

Jarred into action, Boehm dived for the phone, but all he heard was a dial tone. Poor Roxanne. He had to speak to her, had to explain what had happened that morning. There was a coded number that would reconnect him to her, if he could just remember what that was. Star something. Wait a minute – the display on the phone had a menu on it...no good, it was numbers only.

Boehm sank down on the edge of the bed with a sigh. Poor Roxanne and poor Garry Boehm. Hollinger had managed to screw them both with a single phone call.

* * * * *

"There's a damsel in distress minding your quarters for the next few days," Hollinger told Claire as she relieved him of her suitcase and laptop at the door to Boehm's apartment. Following her to the bedroom, which at the moment was for storage, Hollinger inhaled the aroma of tomatoes and oregano and grinned. "Mmm. Whatever you're cooking, it smells good."

"A damsel in distress?" she repeated blankly.

"It seems she was attacked by a mad scientist this morning, and now she's afraid to go home in case he returns with a gun."

Dropping her laptop onto the bed, Claire whirled and stared at him in disbelief. "Are we thinking of the same person?" she asked. "Sophie Hopper, who earlier today tossed me around like a rag doll? And she's afraid to go home? That's ridiculous!"

"I thought so too," Hollinger agreed. "But she seemed sincere about it, so I told her she could move into your place for a while. Do you mind?"

"I guess not," Claire replied with a shrug. "Boy, that's a revelation."

"By the way, she said she'd see you at the meeting tonight. Would you care to expand on that?"

She gasped. "Oh, my God, I'd completely forgotten about that. Damn! And it's the one meeting of the year that I can't miss."

"So go to it," Hollinger told her airily.

"You don't understand. I'm supposed to address the membership tonight. They'll be expecting my body to show up, James. That means you'll have to attend."

He backed away, shaking his head. "I'm developing nervous tics trying to be you with only a couple of people around. Now you want me to go give a speech to a roomful of strangers? Unh-unh."

"Come on, it'll be easy," she coaxed. "I'll print the whole thing out for you. All you'll have to do is read it. Besides," she added, "they're not strangers. They're friends and acquaintances. And Sophie will be there. You just did her a huge favor, James. You were there when she needed me. Trust me, she won't let anything bad happen to you."

"What sort of organization is this?" he asked warily.

"It's called Women for Professional Equity. We're an activist group, monitoring the workplace, lobbying for changes in the labor laws—"

"Unh-unh," he repeated, and folded his arms across his chest.

Just then, there was a knock at the door. Claire heaved a sigh and went to open it.

"You bastard!" Boehm stalked into the living room and stood there for a moment, glowering at Hollinger, the fingers of his right hand flexing ominously around the leather-wrapped handle of a large and heavy suitcase. Finally, he let the bag drop. As it crashed to the floor in the middle of the room, Boehm seethed,

"Do you know what he did? He invited Roxanne to be his date to a very important cocktail party tomorrow night. While she was out shopping for a dress for this affair, he canceled the credit cards she was using. That's his idea of tying up a loose end. You make me ashamed that I'm in your body, Hollinger," Boehm declared, firing each word like a projectile.

The millionaire had gone pale. "You spoke to her?"

"No, unfortunately. She left an angry message on your answering machine."

Claire was struck by a sudden thought. "So, James has a very important social obligation coming up? One he'll need his body to attend, with a date?"

Hollinger groaned. "Claire, please don't do this...."

"It would appear, gentlemen, that what we have here is a *quid pro quo*."

"Oh?" said Boehm.

"Yes," she replied. "James here was being a little difficult about my body attending a meeting of an organization I belong to."

Boehm's eyes widened in disbelief. "But he was so insistent earlier that we all cooperate to fulfill our respective day-to-day obligations."

"Yes. So here is what I propose. If my body doesn't appear at that meeting this evening, then his body ought not to appear at the cocktail party tomorrow night. Fair?"

Boehm nodded sagely. "That seems eminently fair and equitable to me. But let's take it one step further. I think the mind that goes with the body ought to accompany it, to provide guidance in case something unexpected occurs. After all, the point of going to these social functions is to preserve the outward normalcy of our lives as much as possible."

"So that means Claire comes with me to the meeting, and I get to be your date at the cocktail party," Hollinger mused. "Sounds fair to me."

It was Claire's turn to blanch. "Oh, no – Sophie will be chairing the meeting. James, I can't. As soon as she sees Garry's body she'll – she'll destroy it."

"Not if I'm there to protect you, sugar," said Hollinger, grinning smugly. "Remember the huge favor I did her this afternoon...?"

Claire sighed. The reasoning had never sounded so lame. "Maybe I could find a dimly-lit spot in a corner of the room and just stay there. Damn you, James Hollinger!"

* * * * *

At seven-thirty, Claire and Hollinger left for the meeting with fixed smiles on their faces. Claire's was fearlessly clean-shaven -- she'd insisted on wielding the safety razor herself. Boehm hardly noticed their departure. He was remembering Roxanne.

He knew he had no reason to feel guilty. Hollinger was the one who had placed that phone call. And perhaps Hollinger knew best how to deal with a gold-digger, having been so rich for so long. But, gold-digger or not, Roxanne had been Boehm's first. Nothing could dispel the yearning he felt each time her lovely blondness appeared in his mind's eye. Roxanne. Just saying her name to himself was enough to make him ache with longing. And just thinking about the way Hollinger had treated her – and him, come to that – made Boehm want to wring the millionaire's neck.

He was alone in the apartment, his itchings rapidly approaching critical mass. Finally, Boehm snatched a copy of Velikovsky's *Worlds in Collision* from the bookshelf and stalked into the bedroom to sublimate himself in science.

* * * * *

Women for Professional Equity met once a month in the basement of an old church. Hollinger had no idea which church it was. There was no exterior illumination, so he couldn't read the plaque or the sign in front of the building. Claire had even given their destination to the cab driver as an intersection. Now Hollinger stood shivering on the sidewalk, eyeing the gloomy structure uneasily as Claire paid their fare. He couldn't help noticing how much it resembled Castle Frankenstein from the old Boris Karloff movie. If this were a cult film, the audience would be shouting at them right now to get back in the car and escape while they still could. If he were alone, that was precisely what he would do.

"Come on," murmured Claire. "The side door is over here." Hollinger swallowed his heart and followed her.

The church basement was an architect's interpretation of Dante's inferno – a perfectly-constructed brick hearth. A row of castoff wooden chairs lined the front of a makeshift dais, a naked wooden platform several inches off the floor at the end of the room farthest from the oven's maw. More chairs were strung across the room at irregular intervals. Beside him, Hollinger heard Claire's soft gasp of horror. There were only four women there, not the crowd she had been expecting to cover her entrance.

The four women turned together at the sound of footsteps. One of them was Sophie Hopper, and her eyes glinted dangerously as they rested on the face of the man who had accosted her that morning.

Claire began to babble. "Here she comes. She's moving in for the kill."

"Claire, if you run away and leave me here, I swear I'll finish the job for her myself," Hollinger told her through gritted teeth.

"Then do something!" she hissed frantically.

As Sophie approached, Hollinger asked, "Where is everybody? You told me to be here early."

"Yes, because I wanted you to be on time. You're usually

fifteen minutes late, Claire," Sophie scolded, her nose wrinkling with disgust, "how could you bring this...*person* to our meeting?"

"Now, Sophie," said Hollinger, "I'll grant you that—uh—Doctor Boehm here made a poor first impression today—"

"Poor first impression? That's the understatement of the year." The redhead's voice dripped with scorn. "And he claims to be a doctor?"

"Not a medical doctor," Claire corrected her timidly. "A scientist."

"And you figure that gives you license to be eccentric, is that it?"

"Sophie, please!" Hollinger stepped between them. "I only brought Cl – uh, Garry to the meeting because he wanted to apologize."

Claire's jaw dropped in astonishment. "What?" she yelped, an instant before he sank a silencing elbow into her ribs.

"Can we talk privately for a moment?" he asked Sophie, gesturing savagely at Claire to stay put as the fiery-haired amazon led him to a corner of the room.

"All right, talk," Sophie commanded.

"You actually have met Doctor Boehm before, only you couldn't possibly remember him. He was a surgical patient. With the head injuries he'd suffered, his face was mostly bandages. Hell, after the plastic surgeons got through with him even his own mother had trouble recognizing him," Hollinger went on, warming enthusiastically to his story. "But he knew he'd always recognize you, Sophie. You were the kindest nurse on the ward. With his unbandaged eye he used to follow your progress from bed to bed with the medication tray. And he vowed that when he was whole again—"

Sophie quirked a skeptical eyebrow. "This sounds like a bloody soap opera," she commented drily. "Is that really what he told you? Or is the writer in you taking over and embellishing things?"

Hollinger sighed. "All right, here are the facts. You did know him once, but his appearance has changed, drastically. That's why you didn't recognize him when he spoke to you outside your apartment. And the wildness you talked about was simply frustration that he couldn't find a way to twig your memory. He wants to be friends again, Sophie. Won't you give him a second chance?"

Sophie stared intently at the floor for several seconds. "There was a severely-burned young man once," she said slowly, and glanced over to where Claire stood fidgeting near the exit door. "I remember admiring him for his tremendous courage. The treatment was incredibly painful, but he just clenched his teeth and submitted to it without uttering so much as a squeak. He was transferred to a private nursing home on one of my days off and I never saw him again. How did you find this Doctor Boehm, Claire?"

"Well, uh, actually, he found me."

Sophie pursed her lips thoughtfully. "And he told you he'd been my patient and wanted to look me up again? Honey, you are so gullible. However..." A speculative gleam came into her eyes then as the corners of her mouth quirked into a smile. "He is a handsome devil. And I'll bet he's dynamite in bed. He *is* hetero, isn't he?"

Blindsided, Hollinger stammered uncomfortably for several seconds as Sophie continued, "Because I've noticed some mannerisms... no matter. He's one gorgeous hunk of meat. I wouldn't mind taking him for a spin."

"Yes, well, I'll— I'll just tell him that you've forgiven him."

"Well?" Claire demanded as he retreated hastily across the room toward her.

"Sophie no longer hates you," he reported.

She heaved a sigh of relief. "That's good."

"No, it isn't. Now she wants to have your baby."

"She *what*?"

"Well, she didn't actually say that," he confessed, blushing.

"Thank goodness! Exactly what did she say?"

"That you're a handsome devil and probably dynamite in bed. And she wouldn't mind taking you for a spin."

A spin? thought Claire. Great. They could ride the eddy already starting in the pit of her stomach. "That isn't much improvement over wanting to have my baby," she told him shakily. "Oh, God, here she comes. Let's get out of here."

"But what about your speech?" he protested. "I rehearsed it for half an hour."

"Never mind the damned speech! That's all I needed, having my best girlfriend lust after my body."

"It's Boehm's body," he reminded her.

"You wouldn't be smirking like that if it was one of your former drinking buddies making a pass at you right now," Claire hissed.

Suddenly Sophie was beside them. "Doctor Boehm!" she cried, and the warmth in her voice made Claire shudder inwardly. "I do hope you'll stay for our meeting this evening. We'll be discussing pay inequities in various fields. Claire is reporting on the publishing industry, and we'll have representatives from the areas of public service and finance speaking as well. Perhaps you can provide us with some insight into the world of science...?"

Claire's mind and throat seized up together. "Well, I really don't— I mean—"

"There's no need to be nervous, Garry," Sophie said with a laugh, leaning closer and adding in a bedroom voice that threatened to activate Claire's fight-or-flight response, "You don't mind if I call you that, do you? If you'd rather not address the meeting formally, we can discuss it over coffee."

People were starting to arrive. The first three rows of chairs had already filled up, and Sophie had to rush off to greet several new members.

"James," Claire whispered bleakly, "I don't know anything about the world of science."

"So make something up," he told her. "Sophie won't care – she's only interested in biology anyway."

"How can you joke about this?" Claire had a great deal more to say, but she was cut off by a strident voice behind her declaring, "My Lord, there he is! That pervert has infiltrated our meeting!"

From the far end of the room, Sophie yelled, "Mrs. Griesdorf, no!"

And then, suddenly, there were women rushing toward Claire on all sides, their battle cries splitting the air. She only had time to glance helplessly at Hollinger and utter a squeak of protest before everything went dark – again.

* * * * *

Velikovsky's book couldn't quell Boehm's primal urgings, so he'd gone on to even drier, more technical literature. It was no use. He simply couldn't muster the concentration to absorb any of the data that passed before his eyes – his memories of Roxanne kept getting in the way.

Distractedly, he glanced at the clock on the end table in the living room. Eight-thirty. He was stranded here alone, in Hollinger's body, and Claire's meeting could take hours.

Obviously, there was only one thing for him to do. A new pub had opened around the corner. And since these carnal impulses refused to be ignored, perhaps he could drown them instead.

The Ha'penny was a singles bar tailored for a young, swinging clientèle. Its interior was green and amber. The walls were lined with small booths, separated from one another by stained glass partitions, but inviting intrusion from the large open area in the center of the room. The owner, Ewan O'Meara, presided in person at the long stand-up bar. And O'Meara's partner, Gunther Stark, a former heavy-weight wrestler who had competed under the nickname The Teutonic Menace, presided at the door.

Boehm walked in quietly, took a place at the bar and ordered a scotch. Stark had ignored him, for he was well-dressed and obviously sober. But O'Meara did a double-take and waved his partner over excitedly.

"Gunther, do you know who that is?" he hissed into Stark's ear. "Second stool from the end – that's James A. Hollinger. They call him the Wunderkind of Bay Street. He's always mixing with the hoi polloi. I wonder what the hell he's doing all alone in this part of town."

"Maybe he's slumming," Stark replied with a toothy grin.

O'Meara shook his head in puzzlement. "Jeezus, he could buy and sell us ten times over," he murmured. "He's practically an international celebrity. If any of the broads in this place noticed he was here, they'd be all over him in an instant. Better keep an eye out, Gunther – we may have to hide him in a back room."

Meanwhile, oblivious to the conversations going on all around him, Boehm concentrated on downing his drink. His experience with hard liquor was quite limited, for he'd spent his teen years and most of his twenties in single-minded pursuit of scientific knowledge. But now that Roxanne had shown him some of the delights he'd missed by narrowing his sights at such a tender age, why shouldn't he explore the others as well? He'd never in his life been drunk. It ought to be a real experience.

As the scotch whisky burned a path down his throat he thought he felt Roxanne's grip on his thoughts relax a trifle. Encouraged, Boehm ordered another drink, this time a screwdriver.

O'Meara hesitated for a moment. "But, sir," he said respectfully, "you're drinking whisky. Are you sure you want to mix your drinks?"

"Make it with whisky, then," said Boehm with a shrug.

"But orange juice and whisky don't go together."

"Then make it with something else," Boehm told him reasonably. "How about vodka?"

O'Meara sighed. "Drinking vodka right after scotch, you'll be seeing double in no time, Mister—er, sir."

"Perfect," Boehm declared. "That's just what I want."

"You want to get drunk? Why?"

Fixing O'Meara with a stern eye, Boehm slammed his hand down on the bar and said, "Because I'm not myself today, and that's what I've decided to do. Now, are you going to give me that drink or do I have to go somewhere else for it?"

"One moment, sir," O'Meara replied, stepping to the end of the bar where Stark had taken up his post. "Gunther, Mr. Hollinger has come in with the express purpose of tanking up," he said in an undertone. "Why don't you take him into the back room with a bottle of our finest scotch and try to find out what's going on? I'm sure he'd appreciate the privacy, too."

"Sure thing," Stark said, and grinned once more.

O'Meara fetched the bottle out from beneath the bar and placed it in front of their distinguished patron. "Let me get this straight, sir," he said pleasantly. "You're not here to pick up a date or socialize? You're not interested in action – you only want to get drunk?"

"Right."

"In that case, Mr. Stark here will show you to one of our private rooms, where you won't be disturbed."

Boehm made no protest as he was led away from the bar, for the jolt of whisky he'd already consumed was beginning to have its effect. Suffused with warmth, his limbs seeming to float beside his body, he simply could not conceive of anyone intending him any harm at that moment.

Not even the burly, scarfaced man who had taken his arm in such businesslike fashion and was now escorting him into a tiny, windowless room behind the bar.

The room contained a round poker table and a half-dozen chairs. Assisting Boehm into one of the chairs, Stark told him, "Mr. O'Meara believes that serious drinking ought to be done alone. But if you don't mind, I'll just sit with you for a while."

Boehm shrugged. "If you like, sure."

Producing a glass from the inside pocket of his jacket, Stark wiped it and poured the customer a double shot of whisky. Wordlessly he watched Boehm swallow it down, then refilled the glass.

"We're a little curious, Mr. Hollinger," he said. "What brings you to our neck of the woods this evening?"

"I'm chasing oblivion," Boehm sighed, stumbling only slightly over the last word. He was going to have to drink faster, obviously – it was taking him forever to get sloshed.

"Come on," Stark prodded him. "A guy like you trying to lose himself in alcohol? And in a public place?"

Boehm nodded sorrowfully and drained his glass again. He noticed the liquor wasn't burning his throat anymore. Was that good or bad? "There has been a drastic change in my life," he explained.

The scarfaced man looked suddenly attentive. "Oh?"

"Yes. Imagine waking up and discovering that everything you thought was yours now belongs to somebody else. No warning, no apologies. Just ZAP! and it's gone." Why was his tongue growing larger? His name wasn't Pinocchio...

"Wow, that's terrible," the scarfaced man said.

Suddenly Boehm felt deeply moved by this show of sympathy. Tears welled in his eyes. "They wouldn't even let me keep Roxanne," he sighed.

"Who's Roxanne?"

"A blonde... gorgeous... tiny, perfect face... and boobs that you would not believe. He erased her, like some adding mistake. No heart, no feelings. Made a phone call. Now she's gone."

"Roxanne is your girlfriend?"

"Was," Boehm said miserably. "Then, ZAP!"

"I get the picture," Stark told him grimly. "But why aren't you in your fancy penthouse? There's plenty of security there, and privacy."

Boehm shook his head. "I can't hide there. It's the first place they'd look."

Stark's eyes opened wide. "Any chance they might follow you here?" he asked tensely.

"Oh, for sure they will," Boehm replied, thinking of the note he'd left for Hollinger and Claire back at the apartment. "They've never cared about my mind, you know," he added bitterly. "What I know, what I feel, means nothing to them. Cold-hearted bastards... They just want my body in the right place when this is all over."

"Jee-zus!" Stark breathed. "Can you describe any of them, Mr. Hollinger?"

"A man, tall, lotsa blondish hair," said Boehm, concentrating with difficulty on the images of the other two changelings. "And a woman, short, dark hair...red top-thing...knitted, I think. They're together."

"I'd better get you a pot of coffee," Stark declared, scooping up the bottle and the glass and rushing out of the room.

* * * * *

It was ten o'clock. Stark and O'Meara had been waiting tautly for almost an hour while Boehm snoozed quietly on a cot in the back room.

"This is crazy," Stark whispered across the bar. "I think we should call the police."

"And tell them what?" O'Meara snapped. "That James Hollinger came into our establishment to hide from a couple of syndicate hit men, who we expect to see at the door at any minute? They'd never believe that. I hardly believe it myself, for cryin' out loud! Are you absolutely sure that was what he said?"

"Positive."

Swayed by the firmness of Stark's reply, O'Meara sighed, "Well, maybe we've lucked out and he actually managed to shake them before he got here."

"I'm afraid not, Ewan," Stark murmured. "Look over there."

Hollinger and Claire had just entered the pub. As their eyes adjusted to the lighting inside the Ha'penny, they strained to discern some familiar outline of head or hand among the many patrons, but without success.

"I don't see him," Claire said, frowning. "Are you sure you read that note right?"

"I'm positive," Hollinger replied. "Maybe he's somewhere down at the back."

"Are you folks looking for someone?"

Claire had just raised a hand to finger the painful lump Mrs. Griesdorf's purse had raised on the back of her head when this sudden baritone voice at her right elbow made her start and whirl around. "Yes," she said, wincing as the familiar ache flared briefly once more, "a friend who was supposed to meet us here."

"Maybe you've seen him," Hollinger broke in. "A tall fellow, distinguished-looking, dark eyes and hair, graying at the temples...?"

Stark smiled broadly. "You've just described half the men in this place, honey, including the owner."

"Perhaps if we just walked around," Hollinger suggested.

"By all means," said Stark, waving them generously into the dance floor area of the tavern. Then he rushed back to the bar. "It's them, all right," he told O'Meara grimly. "They fit his descriptions to a tee, and they just described him to me. Claimed he was supposed to meet them here. Now will you call the police?"

But O'Meara stood his ground. "No. Let them look around the place. As long as we don't act suspicious they've got no reason to figure we might be hiding him. When they don't see him, they'll leave. After closing time, we'll put him in my car and take him back to my house. Then we'll call the police."

Stark acquiesced with a shrug.

Meanwhile, Hollinger and Claire saw no sign of Boehm anywhere in the tavern.

"Now I'm worried," she said. "It took us a while to find that note. You don't suppose he got giddy and went for a walk or something."

"It's possible. The same impulse that brought him here could as easily have taken him somewhere else."

"Then your body could be anywhere. It could even be lying in some filthy gutter at this very minute," Claire went on with growing agitation.

"What can we do?" demanded Hollinger impatiently. "Call the police? They'd never believe the truth, even if we were dumb enough to tell them. Things would be so much simpler if he were wearing his own body, or yours."

Claire felt her jaw clench but decided to let the insult pass. "Let's go outside," she sighed.

O'Meara had been watching them carefully from behind the bar. "Here they come," he whispered to Stark. "They're leaving, just like I told you."

"What if they want to look in the back rooms?"

"As long as we smile at them and act innocent they've got no reason to look too closely," O'Meara assured him. "In a few hours we'll be home free."

* * * * *

Boehm awakened with the Sahara Desert in his mouth, camel dung and all. So this was what it was like to be drunk? His eyesight was haunted by ghosts. They kept moving things, leaving a series of outlines behind. His skin felt somehow wrong, as though he'd mistakenly grabbed someone else's on his way out the door. His skull was on too tight. It made his brain ache. No, not his brain. Hollinger's brain. Served the bastard right if it was hurting.

Shakily, Boehm pushed himself up off his cot. Oops! His stomach didn't like that. It was doing cartwheels and loop-de-loops. He needed to get home so he could throw up.

Belching mightily, Boehm managed somehow to reach the locked door of the tiny room, which he finally fumbled open on the fourth attempt. He lurched into the narrow hall and around the corner of the bar just in time to spot Hollinger and Claire heading for the street door. Opening his mouth to call out their names, Boehm was dismayed to find that his clouded mind had misplaced them. What could he do? He had to get their attention somehow.

"Hey, you two!" he cried.

They stopped and spun around. "Thank goodness!" Hollinger declared.

As they returned to the middle of the room, however, a heavily-muscled body stepped in front of them, blocking their way. "The exit is behind you," said the bouncer in a quietly menacing voice.

Hollinger and Claire exchanged troubled looks. "But that's our friend," Claire said with a nervous laugh. "The one we came here to meet."

"He's no friend of yours," the ex-wrestler growled.

Hollinger frowned. "That may be true, but it's certainly not your place to say so," he pointed out recklessly. "Now would you mind getting out of our way?"

Claire could see Boehm swaying unsteadily behind this human wall that barred their path. The scientist looked ghastly, and she understood at once that she and Hollinger would have to get to him, since he was obviously incapable of joining them under his own power. Suddenly she had an idea.

"What if we bought this gentleman a drink?" she suggested with what she hoped was an affable smile. But as she reached into a pocket for Boehm's wallet, Claire heard the bouncer suddenly bellow, "I'll save you, Mister Hollinger!"

Startled, she glanced up just in time to see Stark barreling towards her.

Instinctively sidestepping the charge, Claire watched her attacker plow instead into a mixed group who had been standing around a booth holding assorted drinks in their hands. Instantly, people and drinks were mashed together and tossed in an untidy heap inside the booth.

Amid a rising chorus of angry shouts, Claire nudged Hollinger and said, "Let's grab Garry and get the hell out of here."

And as O'Meara rushed to call the police, Claire and Hollinger each took one of Boehm's arms and hustled him out the front door.

* * * * *

By 1:00 a.m. on St. Patrick's Day, the disturbance at the Ha'penny had finally been quelled and the last of the police vehicles was pulling away from the curb. But none of the changelings noticed. They were sound asleep.

James, in Claire's body, lay swathed in blankets on the living room sofa. Boehm's body, it was decided, must occupy the bedroom, within arm's reach of the telephone in case it rang during the night; and as long as Claire's mind was inside that body, she was determined not to share the bed. So, Boehm, in James Hollinger's body, curled up on the carpet behind the sofa, where he lost consciousness and began snoring blissfully almost immediately.

CHAPTER TWELVE

They're entertaining, I'll give them that.

Engrossed in observing the progress of his experiment, Demonai did not notice the intrusion of Olla'set's pod inside the bubble until it nudged his membrane to initiate communication.

Welcome, Aggregator, and thank you for accepting my invitation to join me.

That was no invitation, Demonai – it was a threat, one that I won't soon forget if you can't show me compelling proof that these creatures are truly sentient.

Actually, Aggregator, I meant it as a warning. What you just communicated to me, however – that was a threat.

Demonai, please, begged Tillah, arriving third and joining the meld. *It took considerable persuasion to get Olla'set here. One disrespectful spark from you could undo all my hard work.*

You're right. My apologies, Aggregator.

Tillah has informed me that you are considered a god by the threedees, that you protect some of them and grant their wishes.

Tillah communicates the truth.

Then your collection sac must be uncomfortably full of their tribute.

I don't understand, Aggregator.

You frighten them with your power over them and they bring you offerings of coherent matter. That is tribute, he explained patiently.

That isn't the way I've been doing it, Aggregator.

Then you've been doing it wrong. Let me show you.

Before Demonai could react, Olla'set plunged a secondary pod numerous times into the third-fourth dimension.

There. Temples should already be erected, overflowing with tribute.

What did you do, Aggregator?

I announced myself to a threedee and ordered it to worship me or be disaggregated. Then I appeared to it several times more to convince it of my great power.

Which threedee? demanded Demonai and Tillah in unison.

You wish proof? Fine. It was that one. By my third visit it was telling others about me. Implant yourselves and witness the making of a god.

CHAPTER THIRTEEN

1998

March 23, 3:00 p.m.

"Thank you for agreeing to see me in chambers on such short notice, sir."

Chief Magistrate Cormac "Mack Truck" O'Toole glanced up from the stack of papers on his desk and regarded his visitor narrowly. Round face, almond eyes, nervous hands gripping a brown leather zipper-case. And much too youthful in appearance to convince anyone at first glance that she could be a second-year law student. A high school sophomore, maybe, but even that was pushing it.

"Your petition intrigued me, Ms Perrone," he informed her sternly. "Don't get me wrong. I've seen – and done – my share of law school prankery, and I can smell public mischief all over this. But I admire the boldness and ingenuity you and your accomplices have demonstrated, and I wanted to meet you and tell you that to your face."

The young woman's expression became even more strained. "I'm afraid this isn't a joke, Mr. Chief Magistrate."

"Oh, no?" He read from the first page of the document his secretary had handed him earlier that day. "It says here that you're asking for an injunction against 'Olla'set the Magnificent, Megapotentate of the Twelfth Spatial Dimension'."

"That's just what he calls himself. But he's real, sir, and he poses a genuine threat, not only to my client, but to all of us."

He shot her an incredulous look. O'Toole had checked her

out immediately after receiving her petition. Paulina Perrone might not look it, but she was the real deal – 23 years old, with a Bachelor's degree in History and a year of law school already under her belt. Nonetheless, it was astounding to think that this little thing with the voice of a child and no standing whatever with the Bar Association could actually have a client.

Stubbornly, she continued, "Olla'set claims to be a god. He says that my client, Joseph Nathan Russell, has been neglectful by not paying tribute to him for the past ten years and now owes him 1430 glasses of homogenized milk, or the equivalent value in calcium and silica, plus interest."

"And does he?"

"Sir?"

"Does your client owe someone 1430 glasses of milk?" O'Toole repeated patiently.

"No! This is extortion, plain and simple."

"Hmph." He resumed flipping through the motion in his hands. It bore a clerk's date stamp and initial, meaning it had actually been filed. So the courthouse staff were in on this? Now he *knew* they were getting close to April Fool's Day.

As stated, the purpose of the injunction was twofold: first, to prohibit this self-proclaimed god from harassing Mr. Russell until all claims and charges pertaining to the twelfth spatial dimension had been settled in a terrestrial court; and second, to stop Olla'set from taking any action that might result in the disaggregation of the entire third dimension.

That last was the part that had got Paulina Perrone through the door of his office today. How could he possibly pass up listening to a plea for help to save not the city, or the nation, or even the world, but the whole damned third dimension? What breathtaking, lunatic audacity!

Minute by minute, his conviction grew: there was no way a

second-year law student could have cooked this up by herself. Richard Slattery, the current dean of the law school, had to be involved somehow. The practical jokes he and O'Toole had orchestrated together in their undergraduate years there had been the stuff of legends.

O'Toole put on his grimmest face and motioned her to sit down.

"Tell me, Ms Perrone, how does the twelfth spatial dimension concern my court, exactly?"

She swallowed audibly. "If you'll grant us the injunction, sir, we plan to file criminal charges."

"Oh?"

"Yes, sir. Olla'set's persistent, ongoing harassment of my client caused him to have a serious automobile accident three weeks ago. He just got out of the hospital."

This stunt had Rick Slattery written all over it. It was good to know that nearly thirty years spent immersed in the minutiae of jurisprudence hadn't been able to erode all the brilliant mischief out of him. And it was time for something like this. Slattery had been too quiet, for far too long. Refilling his tank, probably.

"So, you'll be charging Olla'set with...?"

"Criminal harassment and assault causing grievous bodily harm."

"And I presume you'll be seeking damages amounting to 1430 glasses of milk, to cancel out this would-be god's claim?"

To his surprise, the young woman shook her head. "Mr. Russell isn't interested in collecting punitive damages, sir. He just wants Olla'set to back off and leave him alone."

"And not destroy the universe," O'Toole added, no longer able to keep the smile off his face. "This has been a pleasant diversion, Ms Perrone, but I have to get back to my real job now. Be sure to give my regards to Dean Slattery," he added, holding the petition out to her across his desk.

She stiffened in her chair. To her credit, there was steel in her eyes, but he couldn't help noticing that her chin was wobbling. "Would you be taking this more seriously if a member of the bar had presented it to you, sir?" she demanded.

"Absolutely," he assured her. The document dropped forcefully onto his desk top, making a sound like a face being slapped. "Any experienced lawyer who came to me with a tale like this would have been cited for contempt and recommended for disciplinary action within the first two minutes."

"How can I convince you that this is no joke?"

"The usual way, young lady: with arguments and evidence. You do understand the definition of admissible evidence…?"

At that, she got to her feet, snatched up the petition and squared her shoulders. "I'll be back, Mr. Chief Magistrate, with evidence."

Sure, you will, on April Fool's Day, no doubt, he thought, smiling to himself as he watched her march resolutely out the door. As it closed behind her, he punched the intercom key on his desk phone. "Elizabeth," he told his secretary, "get me Dean Slattery at Upper Canada University, Faculty of Law."

Paulina Perrone's visit had triggered an avalanche of memories: the law librarian's Volvo, resting upside-down in the branches of a century-old maple tree; the registrar, staring aghast at his office door which had somehow shrunk overnight to a quarter of its normal height, forcing him to go through it on all fours; five law professors, dumbly looking at the place in the faculty dining room where the kitchen and serving area had been seamlessly replaced by banks of junk food vending machines, also overnight. There had been at least a dozen other pranks, each more insanely brilliant than the last, and all targeting the residents of what Slattery liked to call 'the pompous plane of existence'.

Slattery and O'Toole would imagine the prank together, discuss it, revel in the thought of it for an hour or two. Then,

Slattery would somehow manage to execute it, by himself. Like a magician, he never divulged how he'd done it, not even to his faithful co-conspirator. Whenever O'Toole, dying of curiosity, pressed him for details, Slattery would tell him with a wink, "See, I have this genie trapped inside a bottle." Then they'd have a good laugh, followed by a beer or three at the student pub.

They'd had a lot of good laughs together, before they'd graduated and gone their separate ways. Had it really been 27 years ago? That was far too long a time between laughs, especially now that O'Toole himself was apparently residing on 'the pompous plane of existence'.

* * * * *

Paulina Perrone heaved a discouraged sigh as she dropped her zipper case onto a chair seat and shrugged out of her brown corduroy jacket in the law school refectory. The eating area was almost empty. There were only a handful of students scattered about, most of them hunched over weighty-looking tomes and sipping distractedly out of Tim Hortons coffee cups. One young man, a teaching assistant she recognized, had spread his *Globe and Mail* out over an entire table. He glanced up long enough to wave cheerily at her before plunging back into the Business section.

Oh, to have nothing more to worry about right now than a term paper!

She'd walked all the way from O'Toole's office at the courthouse, trying to think of some relatively painless way to break the bad news to Joey. Unfortunately, no epiphany had struck her en route. All she'd accomplished was to be twenty minutes late for her meeting with her client.

He sat across the table from her now, looking like an Edvard Munch painting with curly blond hair. Hollow eyes, hollow cheeks – and a thigh-high plaster cast on his left leg, which he'd elevated and was resting on the third chair at the small round refectory table. Joey wasn't the only one looking terminally sleep-deprived; it was crunch time for the students at the university, caught between essay deadlines and the looming shadow of final exams. Joey Russell, however, was caught in a much more desperate place. If a light did appear at the end of his tunnel, it would probably turn out to be the train.

He waited patiently for Paulina to hang her jacket neatly across the back of her chair, move the zipper case onto the table and sit down. Then he ventured a question. It was *pro forma* – the expression on her face had already given him the answer.

"Any luck?"

She shook her head sadly. "It's same-old, same-old, kid. Nobody wants to take this seriously. They think I'm playing an early April Fool's joke. O'Toole even told me he thought it was a very good April Fool's joke, and he ought to know. Then he threw technicalities at me – said he wouldn't lift a finger unless I presented him with hard evidence. Has Olla'set bothered you yet today? Hopefully, in front of several reliable witnesses that I can depose?"

"No, sorry."

Nodding philosophically, she accepted the lukewarm coffee that he handed her. Served her right for being late, she thought. "Don't apologize. In my experience, a serious bully doesn't give up. He'll be back." ... *probably with a posse*, she nearly added, but stopped herself just in time. "None of this makes any sense, Joey," she said instead. "I mean, you expect to meet up with his kind in the schoolyard, demanding your lunch money. But years later, inside the toilet tank in your bathroom? Or threatening you at night from under your pillow? And why on Earth would a god want you to hand over every glass of milk you drank after school from fifth grade through twelfth?"

"It wasn't his first choice of tribute."

"What?"

"The first thing he demanded from me was a kilo of diamonds. I was just ten years old at the time, and terrified. If he'd asked for my bike, I would have handed it over. But diamonds? I told him he was being ridiculous, and he left. A month later, he was back, saying that out of the goodness of his heart he would settle for my weight in gold. Again, there was no way. I suggested politely that he go bother someone else for tribute." He paused, looking thoughtful. "That was probably my first mistake – saying 'please'. Anyway, he kept coming back, each time demanding something different – it was as though he was working his way down a list. It took him years to get to calcium, at which point I said, 'You mean milk?'"

"Your second mistake," commented Paulina.

"Yeah. And my third was letting slip that milk was a food, and that all the milk I'd ever drunk was stored in my bones and teeth," he concluded miserably.

"Well, you certainly made it easy for him to terrorize you," she agreed. "But I wouldn't be so quick to beat myself up if I were you. O'Toole said that he could smell public mischief all over this. What if he's onto something?"

Joey's eyes widened, then narrowed. Leaning as far over the table as he could, he hissed vehemently, "It's not a joke, and I'm not crazy."

"I know you're not," she assured him, "but—"

"There has to be someone who will help us," he went on raggedly. "My mom's been after me to see a psychiatrist. If I thought being in a mental hospital would keep Olla'set away from me, I'd commit myself in a minute. I'm just glad you were there that day, Pauly, when he threatened to turn me inside out."

Actually, it hadn't been the threat so much as the way Olla'set had levitated Joey and made the skin and muscle seem to disappear for a moment from his entire left side. All the bones had been fully exposed, and the morbid thought had occurred to her that anyone, including herself, could have touched them, wiggled them, even plucked them right out of his body. Just remembering that moment now was making her a little queasy.

"Yeah, it was lucky that I was there," she agreed uncertainly.

"So what's our next step?"

"Dean Slattery, I guess."

"Great! Another legendary prankster."

"Well, Joey," she sighed, "I don't know what else to do. Maybe this *has* all been some elaborate practical joke, and someone like Dean Slattery can debunk it for us."

CHAPTER FOURTEEN

I don't understand, said Olla'set. *It worked all the other times.*

So you did communicate with the threedees? Demonai said wonderingly.

Not at first. Not by making sound waves. I just shook the ground or exploded a mountain, to see what the creatures would do. Later, I singled out threedees and made my demands to them from various objects. Their reaction was always the same: build a temple, fill it with tribute. That was my *experiment, and I believed it had been successful.*

Well, the threedees are driven to study and understand their reality, Aggregator. Before they knew what caused such things as floods and quakes, they were fearful. They imagined that these disasters must be the work of powerful beings who needed to be appeased. However, the threedees have learned a great deal since then about the nature of their world. They are a lot harder to frighten, and they don't respond well to threats.

And if Olla'set had studied them instead of bullying them, Demonai mused, he would already know that.

The female speaks of 'debunking'. What does that mean?

It means she doesn't believe that you are real, and she hopes the other threedee can help her prove that what you've done is simply an act of mischief by a third threedee.

That's ridiculous! Of course, I'm real!

You persist in denying that they are sentient. Now they plan to use reason and logic to disprove your existence. That seems fair payback to me. Tillah, what do you think?

Wisely, Tillah ignored his question and instead posed one of her own. *Demonai, the 'legendary prankster' the female plans to consult—that wouldn't be...?*

It would. I am his sidekick. I expect he'll be contacting me very soon.

How would he do that? she wondered.

You'll see.

CHAPTER FIFTEEN

1998

March 24, 1:00 a.m.

He was about to let the genie out of the lamp. Again. Richard Slattery had no idea what nearly thiry years of solitary confinement might be like for a supernatural being like Demonai, but he knew how he himself would feel after just a day of it. He would be madder than hell. According to legend, a genie had to obey whoever owned his receptacle, but legends had been known to be wrong. What if Demonai, once freed, turned his powers against his supposed master? Slattery shuddered at the thought, but his resolve held firm. After the phone message from Mac and the story he'd heard that evening from Paulina Perrone, he knew that it was a chance he would have to take.

Wearily, he sank into the brown leather armchair behind the heavy oaken desk in his study and let his gaze wander across the desktop, past the marble pen-holder, the embossed leather CD case, and the half-empty whisky bottle and recently refilled shot glass, to the smudged and tarnished object occupying the middle of an otherwise pristine emerald green desk blotter. The first time he'd seen the lamp, at a flea market in Wasaga Beach, it had looked like something straight out of the Arabian Nights. Now, after all those years it had spent in a straw-filled wooden packing crate in his mother's – now his – attic, it reminded him more of an armor-plated gravy boat.

Slattery glanced sideways at the shot of whisky – his third in the past thirty minutes – and let his lips quirk into a faint, rueful smile. Liquid courage, O'Toole had once called it. Tonight, that was exactly what it was.

For he'd concealed the lamp not to keep it safe from the world, but to keep the world safe from it – or, to be more accurate, safe from the powers possessed by the being it contained. Demonai had made a Volvo fly across a street and land upside-down in the topmost branches of a tree. He'd melted an entire wall of the registrar's office and reshaped it to Slattery's specifications. He could even get inside people's heads, read their thoughts, make them hallucinate according to a script.

Slattery wasn't sure exactly when it was that he'd realized he had a proverbial tiger by the tail. He only knew that he'd awakened one morning in a cold sweat, with the sound of Demonai's laughter ringing in his ears and shreds of a horrific nightmare sliding off the edges of his memory. From that moment on, the very thought of summoning the genie from the lamp was enough to tie his stomach in knots; and the thought of someone else doing it turned the knots into ice. Slattery had channeled Demonai's powers into harmless practical jokes – the lamp's next owner might have plans that weren't nearly as benign. So, wearing thick gardening gloves, he had carried the beautiful old antique up to the attic and 'disappeared' it, for the good of all humankind.

And now it was out of its crate and sitting in the middle of his desk, waiting with a disconcerting air of expectancy for him to work up the nerve to pick it up and stroke its sides. If he was lucky, he wouldn't be destroyed by Demonai the moment the genie emerged. If he wasn't... well, that was what the third shot of whisky was for, to help Slattery get past thoughts like that and do what needed to be done.

Earlier that evening, Paulina Perrone had come knocking on his door with a story about a friend of hers, one Joseph Nathan Russell, who had been living a nightmare for the past ten years with a genie of his own. This genie had a sadistic streak and no lamp to hold him captive. Why he had chosen this particular boy to terrorize, Slattery couldn't even begin to guess. But as he listened to Paulina describe Joseph Russell's situation, a single thought sank bulldog teeth into Slattery and refused to let go: *There are more of them out there!*

He had always assumed, perhaps naively, that there was only one genie in the world, and that he'd prevented Demonai from ever doing any harm by shutting him away in the lamp. Now, learning about a second, 'evil' genie, Slattery was forced to rethink his earlier strategy. Clearly, he would have to release Demonai – sooner rather than later – and pray that 28 years of confinement hadn't turned his 'good' genie into another Olla'set.

Paulina had spoken about injunctions and countersuits. She was an excellent law student, at the top of her class, but she clearly had no idea what they were dealing with, and he couldn't tell her without revealing the existence of the lamp. In fact, he couldn't even let her know that he fully believed her story. Making vague promises to do whatever he could, Slattery had ushered a very discouraged looking Paulina Perrone out of his home. Then he'd fetched the whisky bottle and a shot glass out of his bottom right desk drawer.

All right – he'd wasted enough time.

In one smooth motion, Slattery scooped up the shot glass and swallowed the third whisky. Then he slammed down the empty glass and carefully picked up the lamp.

No longer bright and gleaming, the metal surface felt rough, even a little sticky to the touch. Slattery was glad to be wearing a long-sleeved shirt as he cradled the lamp in the crook of his left arm and began gently stroking its exposed side with his right hand. Three times… four times… nothing.

He felt a sudden chill. What was he doing wrong? Did genies

hibernate? Did they sicken and die of neglect? *Was* there still a genie inside this lamp? Because it would be just like Demonai to let Slattery believe for 28 years that he was imprisoned here when in fact he was— where? Where could Demonai be? Muttering darkly under his breath, Slattery got unsteadily to his feet, still cradling the lamp. A horrible possibility had just occurred to him: What if Demonai and Olla'set were the same being?

"Come on," Slattery growled, trying once more. He took the lamp in his right hand and rubbed its other side, as energetically as he could stomach, with his left. Three times... four times.... still nothing.

Frustrated, Slattery let the lamp drop back onto the desktop and fished around with two fingers in his pants pocket for a tissue to wipe his hands. "Come on out, Demonai," he challenged the air in the room. "Please! You have to tell me what the hell is going on. Who is this Olla'set and where did he come from? Can you help us to deal with him? Demonai, I need you. Show yourself, please!"

* * * * *

What in the name of the Universe is happening to you, Demonai? demanded Olla'set.

Demonai felt the familiar, pleasant shudder begin to cascade through him and knew he would have to wait for it to subside before attempting to communicate. Then another shudder, deeper and stronger than the last, surged from one end of his essence to the other and back, igniting a storm of sparks in all three of the melded beings.

Tillah was alarmed. *Demonai, communicate with us! What is that?*

A secondary pod...Slattery is touching...aah. And the final ripple of sensation flattened and disappeared, somewhere in his midsection.

Disgusting! You don't actually let the threedees— let them TOUCH—? Olla'set was too horrified even to complete the thought. But Demonai couldn't help noticing that the aggregator had made no effort at any point to withdraw from the meld. Clearly there had been some pleasure in the experience for him as well.

No, of course not, Demonai reassured them. *The pod is implanted in an object, and the threedee is touching the object. Well, he's stroking it, actually. It's how I've taught him to contact me.*

Of course, commented Olla'set, *you would teach them that. Excuse me, Aggregator, but I need to answer this call.*

* * * * *

Suddenly, a familiar voice flowed out of the lamp:
Yo, Ricky! Long time, no nothin'. Whassup, bro?

Stunned, Slattery froze in place. These were hardly the wrathful outpourings of a powerful genie who had been kept cooped up, incommunicado, for 28 years. In fact, it sounded as though Demonai had spent a good part of that time doing favors for rappers. Slattery sifted his mind for something intelligent to say and came up completely empty.

The genie sighed audibly.

Oh, right – you're a big shot now. Greetings, Dean Slattery. What can I do for you today?

Slattery could hardly believe this. It was as though no time had passed at all. Perhaps, from Demonai's perspective, none had. Maybe that was one of the perks of being a genie.

This had better not be a crank call, man.

Slattery hastened to reply and heard words tumble out of his mouth in no particular order: "N-no! It isn't, D. I just— I was sure you'd be— Because it's been, what? Twenty-five years? More? And you're not even a little upset that I—? What were you doing in there all that time?" he finally blurted out, feeling a heat in his cheeks that was only partly owing to the whisky.

In the lamp, you mean? Didn't I tell you? That's not the only place I hang out.

Slattery swallowed hard, willing the butterflies in his stomach to quit fluttering and settle down. "So, you... travel around?"

Not really. I'm just sort of everywhere all the time. But you were saying you have a problem?

"A young friend of mine is being harassed by a genie. At least, I think he's a genie – he seems to have the same powers as you do." Slattery took a deep breath and continued, crossing his fingers, "I was hoping that you could have a word with the other genie and...you know...make him stop."

All right, Rick, I'll help your friend. But I want to meet him. When Slattery hesitated, Demonai added, *Hey, the Russell kid already knows my kind exist, so you won't be revealing any secrets. And I want to hear his story for myself.*

"How—?" Slattery's throat slammed shut on the rest of the question. He started over, enunciating each word carefully: "How did you know his name?"

I told you, man – I'm everywhere, all the time.

"Demonai, what exactly are you? And what is Olla'set? Are you the same?"

The genie chuckled, raising the hair at the back of Slattery's neck.

You need to hop on the Internet, Richard.

"I'm serious, D."

So am I. Hop... on... the Internet. And set up a meeting for me with the kid. Ciao, bro.

Silence.

"Demonai?"

More silence. Intrigued now, Slattery booted up his laptop, opened his browser, and keyed in Demonai's name for a search. Moments later, he was staring incredulously at his computer screen.

"Son of a bitch," he murmured. "Worshipped as a deity.... special protector of prostitutes and concubines? Holy shit!"

* * * * *

Did that threedee just insult you, Demonai? Olla'set wanted to know. *Twice?*

If I say yes, does that convince you that he's sentient?

It convinces me that he deserves to be disaggregated for showing disrespect to a higher-order being.

Demonai knew that before Olla'set would even entertain the notion that there might be a higher dimension, he first had to be convinced that the threedees were sentient. Clearly, that wasn't going to be easy.

Demonai, Tillah broke in, *isn't there an experiment in progress that you want to show Olla'set?*

Ah, yes. He had almost forgotten about that. *I'm testing the ability of the threedees to find their way out of a predicament that seems to have no solution,* he explained, guiding the aggregator's pod to the melded essences of the three test subjects.

Olla'set wasn't as impressed as Demonai had hoped he would be.

Really! Asking nonsentient three-dimensional life forms to think their way out of a fifth-dimensional trap is an exercise in futility, Demonai.

But if they were sentient, Aggregator, shouldn't they be able to find a theoretical solution to their shared problem? Tillah pointed out.

Olla'set thought for a while before delivering his response: *Very well. If these creatures were actually to pass Demonai's test, then I would be willing to give some consideration to the idea that they might be sentient.*

It was a beginning.

CHAPTER SIXTEEN

2003

March 17, 9:00 a.m.

Boehm was awakened by the sudden slam of the apartment's front door.

"Goddamned extortionist!" Hollinger fumed, flinging a morning newspaper down on the sofa. "Where's my wallet? I need a hundred dollars."

Claire emerged from the kitchen, where she had been stirring oatmeal with a wooden spoon and monitoring the brewing of about a gallon of coffee. "A hundred bucks for a *Globe and Mail*?" she asked incredulously.

"No, a hundred bucks for Mr. Rosseau, the building superintendent. It seems he just happened to see us come in last night," Hollinger snapped. "He thinks it's deplorable that a man like James Hollinger would go out and get himself publicly wasted and have to be carried back here by two people of opposite gender who are obviously shady characters and may both be gay. He also thinks it's newsworthy. But for an extra C-note, as he put it, he can be persuaded to keep his mouth shut. Isn't that charming?"

As he extracted the two fifty-dollar bills from his wallet, he counted the remaining cash. "We've got almost seven hundred left. That ought to do us for a while, unless Lushwell here gets any more bright ideas that that weasel downstairs can capitalize on." Still grumbling, he dropped the billfold on the end table in the living room and stalked out the door again.

As it crashed shut the second time, Boehm moaned and opened

his bleary eyes on a world that looked like a television screen in need of fine tuning.

"Good morning," Claire greeted him cheerfully. "How's your head?"

"Swollen and throbbing," he replied in a gravelly whisper. "And my tongue needs a shave. And my stomach is sending me poison pen letters. Am I dying?"

"No," she told him with a wry grin. "What you are is mildly hung over. Several cups of black coffee and some rest and you'll be good as new."

She made an unholy din with his coffee cup before dropping it noisily onto the end table. Then, smiling sympathetically, Claire took his arm and helped him to a seat on the couch. As she was handing him the coffee, however, the front door flew open again. "No, not that," said Hollinger. "Tomato juice is the best thing for a hangover."

Resolutely Claire pressed the cup into Boehm's hands. "Black coffee is the traditional remedy," she informed him.

"Why not give him 'a hair of the dog' then?" Hollinger retorted, slamming the door behind him and nearly sending the scientist into spasms.

Boehm's hands were shaking. "Please," he whispered plaintively, "could you make a little less noise?"

"No," said Hollinger, glaring at the cringing figure on the sofa. "After that escapade of yours last night you deserve to suffer. Thanks to you, that leech of a building superintendent just sucked another hundred dollars out of us."

"Out of your wallet, you mean," Claire observed tartly. "Come on, James – you're always boasting about your limitless resources. And now Garry's the one who's hung over and I'm the one who keeps getting beaten up, but you're the one who complains the loudest. Does it really hurt that much to part with some of your money?"

"Besides, it was your idea to stay here and put him on a salary," Boehm put in.

"True, but wouldn't you agree that two hundred dollars a day for doing nothing but mind his own business is a little out of line?" demanded Hollinger. "How about some of that coffee, Claire?"

"Get it yourself," she told him. "I only minister to the infirm and the dying."

Impatiently, Hollinger headed for the kitchen. "I'm curious, Garry," he called out a moment later. "Why did you go to that bar anyway?"

"Roxanne," Boehm muttered miserably.

Hollinger emerged from the kitchen then, stirring his coffee with a clattering spoon that resounded in Boehm's head like Big Ben striking the hour. "Don't tell me you're still pining over her...! You have to remember whose body you're wearing, Garry. I'm a celebrity. People recognize my face. Good Lord, you played right into Rosseau's hands, getting blasted like that last night!"

"It's not only about you, Hollinger," Boehm pointed out, wincing at the loudness of his own voice. "Not that you'd care, of course, about Roxanne or me. It's Number One who counts, right? Well, you're all alone now. Roxanne's washing her hands of you. Of us. Her phone message practically peeled the paint off the walls at the penthouse."

With an exasperated sigh, Hollinger sank slowly into the armchair. "Listen," he said wearily. "Maybe I'm jaded, but to me, Roxanne was just another attractive woman I could take places and show off and then make love to. I had no personal commitment to her, and as far as I knew, she felt the same about me. We dated for fun and for mutual sexual satisfaction. End of story."

"Were you born a sexist pig, James, or did you have to work at it?" Claire interjected.

Hollinger ignored her. Still addressing Boehm, he went on,

"Obviously, in the several hours you spent with Roxanne you established a different sort of rapport. Okay – I can't knock that. You and I are two different people. But as long as you're occupying my body, friend, I'll thank you to indulge your lovesickness in private."

"Listen here, *Mister* Hollinger!" Boehm blustered, livid despite the pallid sheen of his skin. "You're worse than jaded. You're probably the most callous individual I've ever met. Before your despicable lifestyle was thrust upon me I'd never experienced—" His coffee cup was rattling dangerously in its saucer. Claire leaned forward, ready to catch it before it spilled its contents all over Boehm's lap. "I never knew…" Boehm was perspiring with the effort of speaking without throwing up. "…how rotten a man could feel about wanting—"

Suddenly, his face the color and texture of a giant pearl, the scientist leaped off the sofa and headed for the washroom. Claire barely managed to rescue the carpet from a caffeine bath as he rushed past her.

"I was afraid Roxanne might react that way," Hollinger murmured sadly, and heaved a sigh.

"So now what?" Claire wanted to know. "Are you going to go out and get smashed too?"

He seemed to physically shake off the moment. "Don't be ridiculous," he snapped. "In our present condition we can't afford that kind of sentimentality, and Garry's just going to have to realize that. So Roxanne is history. Her choice. Still, it's such a waste."

Disgusted beyond words, Claire leaned back in her seat. But Mrs. Griesdorf's purse had raised a lump the previous morning and the spot was still tender. As it contacted the rear cushion of the sofa Claire winced and clapped a hand to her head. "That old lady must have been carrying bricks in her purse," she moaned. "What happened after I passed out, anyway?"

Hollinger shrugged. "Just what I told you before. There were maybe two dozen women there, and they obviously had never seen a man faint before, because they stood around and gawked at you as though you were an Egyptian mummy on display at the museum."

"And Sophie didn't—?"

He grinned. "Ravish your unconscious body? No. After a few minutes she offered to call an ambulance, and if you hadn't stirred and opened your eyes just then, I might have said yes. End of story."

"I fainted," she repeated, picking at the memory as though at a scab. "That is so embarrassing."

"Why? Women faint all the time."

"No, they don't. They used to, because their corsets were so damned tight they couldn't breathe. Am I wearing whalebone? No. Am I trying to have a twelve-inch waist? No! Do I want to be seen as a sexist cliché? No, no, no!"

"Did you just stamp your foot?"

"One more word, Hollinger, and you're dead."

"I'm in your body," he reminded her. "You could kill my body, but then you'd be killing Garry."

"Don't tempt me," she muttered. "He's the reason I was even at that meeting last night. All that research I did about pay scales in the publishing industry, and you didn't even get to deliver the speech."

Just then Boehm reappeared, still ashen but looking more composed than he had been when he left the room. And the telephone began to shrill. For several seconds they all stared dumbly at it, until Hollinger sighed, "Claire, you've got the voice that belongs with the apartment. You'd better answer it."

Warily she picked up the receiver. "Hello? Yes, this is Doctor

Boehm," she said in her most formal tone. Suddenly her eyes widened and began glancing about in panic. "Why, Sophie! Ha, ha! What a surprise!"

Hollinger groaned and buried his face in his hands. Maybe he *was* a sexist pig, but there was no denying the fact that they wouldn't be having this problem if Sophie Hopper were an old-fashioned, unliberated woman.

"Don't be silly. It did not take courage." Claire's face assumed a martyred expression. "Oh, you did? That was very ingenious. No, I wasn't expecting your call – it took me completely by surprise." Covering the mouthpiece of the receiver with one hand, Claire whispered beseechingly at Hollinger, "Can't you do something about this?"

Helpless, he merely shrugged.

"Good grief!" Claire exclaimed into the telephone. "No, I— I didn't know that. Ha, ha! No, I'm not."

All at once Claire was on her feet, her free hand flapping excitedly in the air. "No, you'd better not," she stammered, the color rising in her cheeks. "No, really. Well, I'm not decent. I'm warning you, don't! Sophie, if you set one foot in here before I'm ready to see you, I'll—"

Now she was prancing from one foot to the other, like a child with a full bladder. It would have been an amusing enough sight had she been in her own body, but as he watched her perform this dance with Boehm's long legs, Hollinger had to work hard to contain his laughter.

"No, I'm not angry wi— Yes! I'm furious! No, I don't want you to come over and apologize. No! Absolutely not!" A pause, then Claire moaned, "Oh, Lord, don't cry. All right, I forgive you. Yes. No! Well, maybe some other time. Okay. Goodbye."

Lips tightly compressed, a smudge of flaming color on each of Boehm's cheekbones, Claire hung up the receiver. "How the hell," she asked coldly, "did she get this phone number?"

Hollinger carefully recomposed his features and wiped every trace of merriment from his voice before replying.

"From the phone book, probably," he said with another artless shrug. "How many Boehms can there be in the Toronto directory?"

Claire's face fell. She looked on the verge of tears. "The directory? There are street addresses in the directory. Oh, my God, she knows where to find me."

"What's so terrible about that?" Boehm asked.

"You've heard of phone sex? This was phone rape," she declared.

"All right, all right, just simmer down," said Hollinger. "Sophie isn't a barbarian, you know. Green belt and all, she was frightened of you earlier, remember?"

"Sure, but that was before she decided to have my baby," Claire protested shrilly.

Hollinger threw his hands up in exasperation. "She never said that – I did," he cried. "I was rattled. I paraphrased poorly. Okay?"

Puzzled, Boehm interrupted, "I don't see what everyone's getting so excited about. I mean, what's this Sophie going to do? Kick down the door and carry you off like King Kong?"

Hollinger and Claire answered him simultaneously:

"Of course not!"

"Quite possibly!"

"Well, since we're all going to be here together, why worry about it?" Boehm asked. "James and I can protect you, Claire."

Struck by a sudden thought, Hollinger winced. "Except for tonight," he said, looking pained.

"What? What are you talking about?" she demanded nervously.

"The cocktail party. It's this evening. I'm afraid you're going to have to stay here alone for a couple of hours."

Claire's face went nearly as pale as Boehm's had been earlier.

"You can't do this to me," she rasped. "It's inhuman!"

"Look," he went on consolingly, "it's only for a short time—"

"But she has this address!"

"But she's not a psychic. How is she going to know you're alone?"

If he'd been in someone else's body, Claire would have throttled him for being both sexist *and* obtuse.

"Wrong!" she exclaimed. "Unless she's a psychic she's going to *assume* that I'm alone, dammit!"

Hollinger's smile faded. "Oh."

"I'll visit the Ha'penny and get bombed out of my skull," she warned.

But he only shook his head. "You'll visit the Ha'penny and get beaten up again. Bouncers are known for having long memories."

Claire sank back in her seat with a faint moan.

"Listen, Claire, there's nothing to be afraid of," said Boehm. "All you have to do is lock the door behind us when we leave and pretend the apartment is empty. Don't answer the phone, don't turn on any lights—"

"Sit here in the dark until you two decide to come home from the party? Thanks a lot."

"You haven't much choice," Hollinger reminded her. "This party is as important to me as your meeting was to you. And if we suddenly fail to honor our commitments, somebody is liable to put two and two together and get twenty-two. It's bad enough that we're paying Rosseau to keep his mouth shut about us—"

Incensed, Claire leaped to her feet. "Can't you ever forget about your wallet?"

"He's right, Claire," said Boehm. "It only takes one informant to make us front page news."

Heaving a defeated sigh, Claire muttered, "All right, I'm convinced. But I don't have to like it."

The rest of the morning passed relatively uneventfully. After tasting Claire's lumpy oatmeal concoction – which brought back memories of the flour-and-water paste his mother often made for him to play with when he was a child – Boehm insisted on preparing lunch, to Hollinger's great relief. Claire hadn't liked breakfast any better than they had; she turned over the kitchen to him without argument. Besides, she had almost finished writing that short story for Ralph Ignace and wanted to spend a few hours on her computer.

Fortunately, the laptop had a full-sized keyboard. Claire's work proceeded slowly at first as she directed Boehm's large hands over the keys. But within half an hour she was touch-typing as steadily as ever.

Ralph was going to love this story. It oozed sensuality. The prose was as purple as a fresh bruise. The sex scenes were explicit but tasteful. Best of all, it was completed by half past eleven, in plenty of time to be taken to the post office for next day delivery.

"Would you like me to drop that off at your publisher?"

She swiveled her chair and saw Hollinger leaning against the doorjamb.

"Lunch won't be ready for an hour, I've read all the magazines I can understand, and there's nothing worth watching on the tube," he explained. "I need to get out for a while."

Frowning, Claire jogged up the printout of the story and fastened the pages together with a paper clip. "I don't think that's a good idea, James," she told him. "Let's just slip this into an envelope and mail it to him."

"Snail mail? That's silly," he protested.

"I agree, but it's the way Ralph prefers to receive submissions. And in this case, it's the safest way to send them."

"Safest how? If his office were in Iqaluit or Yellowknife I would understand, but it's right here in Toronto. Why risk having your story go astray in the mail and take days or even weeks to arrive when I can have it on his desk within the hour?"

Claire looked torn. Finally she sighed and said, "Have a seat, James, and let me tell you something about Ralph Ignace."

Intrigued, Hollinger sat down on the foot of the bed.

"He's never betrayed me professionally, but on a personal level…" She paused, visibly steeling herself, then went on, "Ralph Ignace is the 'dirty' in 'dirty old man' personified. It's the nature of his business. He's a porn publisher. Every time we've met face to face, he's undressed me with his eyes. And it isn't just me. I'm told he does that to every woman he sees. The man has delusions of Hefnerhood. There's also an unconfirmed rumor in the industry that his desk converts into a heart-shaped bed at the push of a button. And while he's never actually been charged with sexual assault, that doesn't mean he hasn't tried it. Now, are you sure you want to take him this manuscript in person? As you told Garry this morning, please remember whose body you're wearing."

Briefly recalling the last time the Harrington-Smythes had paid him a visit, Hollinger shifted uncomfortably inside Claire's petite frame. But this situation was in no way the same, he told himself sternly. Different office, different body, and no reason to feel he had to stick around if things became unpleasant. "Not to worry, I'll be a moving target, just drop the story off – in and out in a couple of seconds." Then, noticing Claire's skeptical expression, he added, "Doesn't Ignace have a receptionist?"

"Yes. His nickname is Pimperella."

Hollinger paused, visualizing a shiny-haired creature in a purple sequined jacket with huge padded shoulders. Purple. It *would* be purple. He shuddered, and the moment passed.

"Okay, then," he resumed, "I'll leave it with the receptionist. Ignace won't even know I've been there until I've gone. Okay?"

"I guess," she replied uncertainly.

"Hey, it'll be all right," said Hollinger with a grin. "Your virtue will be safe, I promise. Just think of this as part of the adventure."

She managed a faint smile. Adventure? It was turning into a nightmare.

* * * * *

"Ye-es?"

'Pimperella' turned out to be a tall, thin man with a long narrow head. He was impeccably clad in a three-piece brown suit, and so firmly ensconced in the zebra-striped outer office that every syllable he uttered sounded smug and patronizing. Hollinger had never before been looked down on by someone whose eyes were a foot and a half below his own, and he found the experience unsettling. Now, confronting that supercilious stare across a gleaming cherrywood desk, he had to suppress the urge to turn and bolt out the door.

"This is for Mr. Ignace," he managed to say. "Please see that he gets it."

But as Hollinger dropped the manuscript on the receptionist's desk, the door to his right flew open, and a man who strikingly resembled a huge, cuddly teddy bear strode into the outer office. The receptionist greeted him with a broad, knowing smile.

"Nonsense, Claire!" the man declared, placing paw-like hands on Hollinger's shoulders. "I hardly ever see you anymore. Come in for a cup of coffee and let's discuss your next assignment."

"No, sorry, I can't," Hollinger demurred, his skin crawling at the overly-familiar touch. "I'm really in a hurry."

Ralph Ignace licked his lips. "This will only take a minute," he said, drawing the protesting victim into his lair.

Hollinger realized, too late, that he should have heeded Claire's warnings about this man. Ralph Ignace's office was broadloomed right up to the ceiling with green shag and liberally ornamented with the skins of wild animals, mostly predators, arranged so that visitors saw them out of the corner of one eye. The subtle intimations of danger in this mini-jungle would have been enough to psych out anybody who wandered in; but something told Hollinger that these special effects were aimed directly at the female of the species.

Swallowing hard, he repeated, "I really can't stay."

"Of course," Ignace agreed. "Won't you have a seat?" His voice seemed to ooze out of some hot, wet place deep inside him. Involuntarily, Hollinger began to fidget. He'd been propositioned more than once in those same moist tones, by Euphonia Harrington-Smythe. It wasn't a memory he liked to revisit.

"If you hand-delivered this, you must really need the money. Stick around while I read it and I'll cut you a cheque to take with you." Those were the words coming out of Ignace's mouth. Meanwhile, his eyes and body language were saying, *Let me make you warm and pliant, maybe cloud your judgement with a little something extra in the coffee...*

"No, I'm sorry," Hollinger stammered, "I really have to be going."

Ignace sighed regretfully. "Well, I'm sure the quality of this piece will be just as good as your previous work. You really are an excellent writer, Claire. I can have the cheque ready by this evening." The publisher leaned forward on his elbows and intimated sibilantly, "You know how I hate to entrust money to the post office. Why don't I just drop it by your place tonight on my way home? That would be simplest."

"Sure, why not?" Racing wildly, Hollinger's thoughts were a blur. "I think I'd better go now."

"Of course, my dear. I'll see you tonight, then." That quicksand voice followed Hollinger as he scurried past the smirking receptionist and out the door to the street.

Not until he was blocks away from the office building did

he stop to realize what he'd done in that moment of mindless haste – he'd invited wet-eyed, lip-licking Ralph Ignace to visit Claire that evening. Dear Lord, she would kill him! She'd warned Hollinger about Ignace, but he'd refused to listen. And now that repulsive man was going to turn up, expecting sex in exchange for the cheque that was rightfully hers.

But – wait a minute – Ignace couldn't possibly have Boehm's address. That meant he would go to the rooming house in the Beaches, where his knock at the door would be answered by Sophie, the green belt in judo who didn't like strange men making passes at her.

Oh, to be a fly on the atrocious purple wall…

* * * * *

"James, is that you?"

He almost didn't answer Claire's question, for he'd just let himself into the locked apartment with Boehm's key, and not even Rosseau, the sleazebag super, had the gall to enter without knocking first. "Yes, it's me," he finally replied.

"You'd better grab some lunch, and don't dawdle over it. We have to go out this afternoon," she called from the bedroom.

"What? Why?" he demanded.

Claire stalked into the living room then, a study in disgust. "If my body is going to a ritzy cocktail party tonight, then it needs something appropriate to wear. I hate to spring this on you, James, but all I've got in either closet right now is casual stuff. If you don't want to embarrass yourself and Garry this evening, then you'd better grab your credit cards and take us shopping. That's assuming you still have one or two that work…?"

Stung by the reminder of what he'd done to Roxanne, Hollinger pulled himself up to his current full five-foot-three and replied haughtily, "Of course, I do. Do you mind if I have a bite to eat first?"

"Not at all. You can make yourself a sandwich – there's filling in a bowl in the fridge. But you'd better be ready to roll in half an hour. I've already called for the cab."

They were all the same, he thought sourly, striding into the kitchen and swinging the fridge door wide. All they saw when they looked at him was the money. All they needed from him, all they wanted from him, was the money. And he'd tried to be accommodating. He'd gone to that damned meeting, risked life, limb and virtue in the wild beast's den to deliver her stupid story... Where the hell was that sandwich filling?

He straightened with a sigh and opened his mouth to ask someone, then thought better of it. No, they'd probably just take advantage of the opportunity to point out another of his many faults. He'd never imagined the list could be so long. Well, without money, what else could they be right now but self-righteous?

There had to be half a dozen margarine tubs in this refrigerator. Either Boehm was an oleo hoarder, or— There it was. It would have been nice if he'd labeled the damned thing, but that was probably too much to expect from a scientist. Chicken salad, using flaked meat from a tin. It figured. Boehm had chopped celery into it, at least. Thank heaven for small mercies. They'd left him some whole wheat bread, too. Now he just had to find a margarine container that actually held margarine, so he could make his sandwich.

"Hurry up, James. The taxi will be here in fifteen minutes," Claire scolded.

Yeah, yeah. The problem with being in a woman's body, Hollinger decided, was that he had no control, of anything. Boehm had James Hollinger's body and with it everything that gave him his power: his voice, his fingerprints, his presence, and his signature. And even though Hollinger was currently occupying Claire's body, he clearly wasn't running it. Claire was. She was bossing everybody around. So if he didn't control the body he owned, and couldn't control the body he was in, what the hell was Hollinger doing here, besides feeling trapped and helpless and—

Frustrated, he slammed the fridge door shut.

"Hey!" yelped a familiar voice from the other room. "Don't break my furniture!"

"Sorry." Then he said it again, more quietly. "I'm sorry."

He wasn't apologizing to Boehm, Hollinger realized, but to Roxanne. She hadn't deserved the way he'd treated her. She'd come to expect that they would attend the Rockaways' gala together, and that he would pay for a new dress for the occasion. After seven years, the Rockaways and their guests had come to expect it as well. This year, for the first time, his body would be showing up at the party without her. Of course, if he ticked Claire off badly enough, there was a good chance that it might also show up without *him*.

"Come on, people," bawled Claire. "Our ride is here."

As they piled into the cab, she told the driver, "Carewe's, please."

In spite of himself, Hollinger was impressed. This lady might not be able to afford designer clothing, but she certainly knew where to purchase it.

Carewe's, in Yorkville, was a transplant from Rodeo Drive in Beverly Hills. The simplicity of its exterior was deceptive. In the two modest display windows, three or four pantsuits had been tastefully arranged without the use of plaster mannequins, and only the absence of price tags suggested that they might be at all expensive.

The interior of the store, however, was an entirely different breed of retail environment. Claire braced herself as she stepped through the door. Carpeted risers, tiered platforms, gilded archways – it looked like the stage setting of a Broadway musical.

Busby Berkeley would have loved it. But each time Claire set foot in this place, all she could think about was the criminal waste of space.

Usually, she came in with Sophie. The first time, they had wandered in out of curiosity while window shopping. On subsequent visits, they had amused themselves by indulgently deploring the excesses of the very rich. After all, who but an inbred wastrel would spend over two hundred dollars on a plain white cotton blouse with a shawl collar and a Givenchy label at the back of the neck? When they'd tired of tut-tutting the exorbitant prices, she and Sophie would turn critical eyes to the layout of the boutique, the arrangement of the merchandise, the attitudes of the sales staff, and always found Carewe's wanting in all three areas.

As far as she was concerned, they still left something to be desired. The store resembled an obstacle course, there was a ridiculous lack of goods on display and an elegantly-attired saleswoman stared at the three new arrivals in wary disbelief.

It didn't take a rocket scientist to figure out why. Claire was about to prompt Boehm to identify himself when Hollinger suddenly giggled sophomorically and took his arm. Evidently, he hoped that the woman would notice the famous Hollinger face and, realizing that High Finance had entered her establishment, be appropriately awed.

Awed or not, the saleswoman strode across the store toward them, wearing an efficient smile. An instant before she came within hearing range, Claire reminded Boehm in a hoarse whisper, "Ask to see their line of cocktail dresses."

"I know," he muttered irritably. "I'm not stupid."

The woman stopped at what seemed to Claire an excessive distance away. "Mr. Hollinger?" she said expectantly.

"Er...yes," Boehm replied. "I'd like to purchase a fancy cocktail dress for my friend."

Her gaze swept rapidly from the giggling female clamped to the Hollinger arm over to the tall stern-faced man who appeared to be overseeing the proceedings. "Very good, sir." And to Claire's relief, the saleswoman subsided back into brisk officiousness. "Please follow me and I'll have several dresses modeled for you."

At the rear of the store was a small circular stage surrounded by dainty white wrought-iron benches with pink silk seat cushions. Inviting them to sit, the woman disappeared behind a set of matching pink curtains, presumably to issue instructions to a platoon of models kept idling there. Scant minutes later, the fashion show began.

This was what Carewe's was all about: not the sparse arrangement of lifeless garments on the few counters out front, Claire suddenly realized, but this parade of pencil-slim mannequins wearing elegant creations that most women could only dream of owning. She fairly drooled as the models strolled past wearing wrapped satin, georgette studded with cultured pearls, silk jersey that glowed richly under the fluorescent lights – the saleswoman referred to them offhandedly as "frocks", but Claire knew that not a single dress in the line could be bought for less than a thousand dollars.

After a dozen garments had been shown, the saleswoman asked, "Do any of these appeal to you, Mister Hollinger?"

Claire had loved them all. She bit back a disappointed exclamation when James suddenly piped up, "Do you have something a little... simpler?"

Blinking with bewilderment, the woman turned to Boehm. "I've just shown you our most exclusive designer fashions, sir," she pointed out nervously. "And you don't like any of them?"

Once more, 'Hollinger' remained silent and it was the woman at his elbow who replied, "They're all very nice, but we want something a little less eye-catching."

The saleswoman nodded knowingly. "You mean less expensive," she said, her voice tinged with disdain.

James smiled brightly at her. "If those are the simpler dresses, yes. Show us your second-best line."

Eyebrows raised, the saleswoman looked to Boehm for confirmation of this request. He nodded vigorously and said, "I wouldn't mind seeing a few more."

"Of course, sir," the woman sighed, and retreated behind the curtains once again.

Claire took advantage of her withdrawal to berate both men in whispers. "Are you crazy? They're gorgeous! Any one of them would knock a roomful of jet-set snobs dead," she shrieked under her breath.

"I don't want to knock anybody dead," James shouted quietly at her over his shoulder. "Our behavior is going to be eccentric as it is. There's no point in attracting undue attention by showing up in 'an exclusive designer fashion' that'll have all the women and half the men simpering unbearably for weeks afterward."

"And you think underdressing for this affair won't attract undue attention?" Claire demanded, by now thoroughly exasperated.

"Simplicity can be very elegant, Claire," he pointed out. "Now, since I'm buying and I'm wearing, then I'm also having the final say."

"But—!"

"That's enough, you two," Boehm muttered urgently.

All at once, Claire realized that the saleswoman was back, smiling expectantly and flexing her fingers like a teacher waiting for an unruly class to notice her presence and come to order. "You'd better turn around, James," she whispered. "I think the fashion show is about to resume."

Standing at center stage, the saleswoman grinned smugly at them. "We have three short gowns that might suit your needs, from our lower-priced line. Suzanne?" she called.

The first model appeared in pale blue silk jersey with a handkerchief hem and a neckline that dipped almost to her navel. Wordlessly, James shook his head and the mannequin whirled and disappeared behind the curtain.

The second dress was pink, with long sleeves slit from shoulder to wrist and teardrop-shaped openings in the sides of the bodice, exposing plenty of ribcage. Boehm smiled eagerly as the model approached his bench, but James muttered just loudly enough to be heard, "No way!" Then he added, as a reminder to Boehm, "It's the dress we're buying, not the girl inside it."

"Oh," said Boehm, his smile rapidly fading.

Claire prayed that the last dress would be acceptable. It would be mortifying to have to request a showing of their "third-best" line and be informed frostily that Sears was having a sale that week.

The third model, named Starlight, came out in a white silk toga with a purple border. The dress was cinched tightly around the waist, falling in elegant pleats from the hips to just below the knees. It shimmered pristinely as she took long, feline steps toward them.

"That one!" exclaimed Hollinger and Boehm at the same instant.

Starlight wheeled around, revealing nothing but purple lacing holding the bodice of the dress together at the back.

The two men exchanged a dismayed look. Then Hollinger shrugged and said with a nervous little laugh, "So, I'll find a warm wall and keep my back to it."

As the saleswoman turned for a moment to speak to the model, Claire leaned over and prompted Boehm, "Now we need a matching wrap and shoes and a handbag."

Numbly, he nodded. But when the saleswoman came over she didn't give him a chance to speak.

"And what size is your friend, Mister Hollinger?" she asked briskly.

Silence. Claire cringed inwardly for several seconds as Boehm groped for a likely number. Then, with disarming candor, he replied, "I really don't know. Perhaps she ought to try the dress on and see."

Claire's relief was short-lived, for the woman turned to James next and said, "That's a good idea. What size do you usually take, dear?"

Here it comes, Claire thought dully. *He'll turn to me and ask what size he wears.*

But he surprised her. With remarkable presence of mind he smiled up at the woman and returned the question:

"What size would *you* say I should try on?"

"How about an eight?" the saleswoman suggested.

"Fine," he replied, bouncing to his feet. "And I should probably have a wrap to go with that, and some shoes and a bag..." And, chatting animatedly, Hollinger and the saleswoman strolled behind the curtains, leaving Claire and Boehm sitting slack-jawed on their respective wrought-iron benches.

"He's certainly getting into the spirit of things," Boehm remarked faintly.

Claire just nodded and sighed. Now, if only she could enjoy being a man as much as Hollinger seemed to enjoy being a woman.

* * * * *

Are you certain these threedees are even aware of the problem you have posed them, Demonai? They don't seem to be paying it much attention.

They have to work their way through other, smaller problems first, Aggregator. Be patient, please.

Don't even think about making contact with any of them, Olla'set warned. *I heard the hints you dropped to your sidekick earlier.* '*I'm everywhere, all the time. Hop on the Internet.*' *If you violate the integrity of this experiment I'll disaggregate the bubble with you inside of it. Is that understood?*

Understood, Aggregator.

Demonai was confident the experiment would succeed. Threedees were constantly learning. And he had already witnessed during his association with Richard Slattery what a talent they had for getting themselves in and out of trouble, without any assistance from a being such as himself. The three that he had melded were intelligent and would soon figure out who was responsible for the startling change in their lives, because that was how he had originally set things up.

Now he just had to keep Olla'set from realizing that the game was rigged in the threedees' favor.

CHAPTER SEVENTEEN

2003

Still March 17, 7:00 p.m.

Located on the Bridle Path, where homes worth millions of dollars hid coyly from curious eyes behind artfully-placed greenery, Hugh Rockaway's mansion was a showpiece. It flaunted itself. Rather than conforming to his neighbors' tastes and giving it a thousand-foot, tree-lined driveway, Rockaway had had his house constructed so close to the road that it was sometimes mistaken for a public building. But that was typical of the man. Half his acquaintances admired his panache, while the other half condemned him for being tacky and gauche.

Tacky or not, Hugh Rockaway was worth at least fifty million dollars, thanks to an enterprising spirit and James Hollinger's good advice. And he'd returned the favor many times over, with referrals and recommendations that had built Hollinger's firm into a powerhouse.

Twice a year, June Rockaway showed off her dream home at an exclusive social gathering: in the spring, she threw a gala cocktail party for a hundred selected guests; and in the fall, she hosted a lavish costume ball. It was deemed a great honor to receive an invitation to one of these two annual affairs, and something lower than philistine to decline or ignore it. And that was why, come hell or high water, James Hollinger's body, with date, had to show up at the Rockaway mansion between six-thirty and eight o'clock that evening, prepared to consume its share of alcohol and *hors-d'oeuvres* and converse politely for some respectable length of time before taking its leave.

As their taxicab pulled into the wide semicircular driveway that fronted Rockaway's stately gray brick home, Hollinger adjusted his stole and prayed fervently that Claire wouldn't do anything rash while they were gone.

Boehm was preoccupied as well, but for a different reason. Hollinger had force-fed about fifty names and physical descriptions into the scientist's memory, and it took all his concentration to prevent them from coalescing into a single amorphous identity. As his 'date' nervously tugged at the white satin wrap for the hundredth time, Boehm sighed irritably, "You look just fine. Relax."

"I'm not worried about me," said Hollinger. "I'm worried about you. Can you remember all the information I gave you about the other guests?"

Boehm cast a beseeching glance skyward. "Probably not," he replied tightly, "but I think I've learned enough to get by."

Shifting uneasily in his seat, Hollinger groaned inwardly. Perhaps he would have been better off forgetting about this evening after all.

A uniformed attendant opened the cab door for them. Boehm stood gazing up an Everest-like climb to the mansion's front door and felt his mouth go dry. What on Earth had he been thinking? It was one thing to pretend to be James Hollinger for a bunch of faceless strangers, but to do it at a cocktail party, among Hollinger's own friends and business associates—! Nor was Boehm's confidence boosted by the peculiar effect surrounding the Rockaways' front door. Each time it was opened to admit guests, the light that spilled into the deepening night made it glow like the maw of a blast furnace.

"Come on, Garry, buck up," Hollinger whispered encouragingly as he took Boehm's arm and led him toward the hell's-mouth at the top of the stairs. "We're in this together, you know."

Of course they were. Boehm suppressed a smile. The Dunberrys of the world, the dabblers, the sheep – those were the types who needed to flock together to do things. They 'teamed up'. They provided 'collegial support'. They were pathetic. A true scientist didn't need a cheering section or a chorus to be successful. Or a social calendar filled with 'events'. Or—

He paused, recalling the time spent with Roxanne. He might just make an exception for her. She'd taught him a lot about applied biophysics.

Strictly speaking, however, none of that was necessary to scientific discovery. Pure science happened in out-of-the-way corners; and a true scientist needed only to stay focused on those corners, carefully adjust the conditions, and wait. In science as in any other field of endeavor, the most artful hunters worked alone.

Boehm hated to admit it, but he and Hollinger were alike in that respect, the one in pursuit of knowledge and the other in pursuit of profit. The difference, of course, was that people in power wanted people like Hollinger to be successful. Given a choice between funding a series of theoretical physics experiments and underwriting a potentially lucrative investment, the bankers and government types almost always chose the latter.

Boehm cast a glance at the smiling young woman on his arm. How he envied James Hollinger at that moment, pantyhose, mascara and all!

All at once, they were inside the door and being announced by a young man in green livery: "Mister James Hollinger and Miss Claire Smith."

Boehm started. "What? Why did you –?"

Still smiling, Hollinger seized the scientist's arm and pulled him into the huge salon, where tray-bearing servers navigated adroitly between clusters of guests, offering them glasses of champagne and finger-sized delicacies. Not until they were standing on one of Mrs. Rockaway's prized Persian rugs holding drinks and *hors-d'oeuvres* in their hands did he whisper an explanation: "I don't want anyone taking a fancy to Claire and tracking her down the way Sophie did you. There are a thousand Smiths in the phone book but not too many Amorys."

Still unconvinced, Boehm nonetheless smiled and shrugged noncommitally. There was no point in arguing when he needed to concentrate on remembering.

A glance around the room showed him many of the people James had described to him back at the apartment. Bits of that interminable discussion repeated on Boehm like raw onions as his eyes alighted first on the Drysdales, Howard and Marie – "owners of a large meat-packing operation...be sarcastic if you talk to them at all...we don't get along" – then on Doris Plisker, an overblown, overweight kewpie doll – "loaded with affectations... wants desperately to be 'with it' but won't relax and let her natural charm come out... she was a different girl when her husband was alive... maybe that's why she still gets invited to these dos..." – then on Richard Slattery, an angular, distracted-looking man with a shock of graying hair and wire-rimmed glasses, and a wooden pipe hanging off his lip – "the brother-in-law... an academic who couldn't cut it in the courtroom, but he's apparently a genius at getting things done, so they made him dean of the Faculty of Law at Upper Canada University... Hugh says he gives the event 'gravitas', although why a purely social event would need academic weight is beyond me..."

"Da-a-ahling!"

Startled, Boehm nearly dropped his samosa. A statuesque woman with carefully-sculpted bleached-blond hair was swooping down on him, in a blue dress that even sported a wing effect, arms outstretched in obvious expectation of a big, insincere hug. He searched his memory frantically for a second. James had described this person to him. Now who the hell was she?

"That's your hostess, June Rockaway," Hollinger hissed beside him, and all at once everything came back. This was Hugh Rockaway's third wife, the one who was into charity work and who spent most of her vacations with her widowed sister on Majorca.

"Jimmy," she reproached him fondly. "Sally is going to be terribly disappointed that you've brought a date. She's been telling everyone how she intends to monopolize you this evening." Boehm must have looked distressed, for Hollinger patted him reassuringly on the arm as their hostess burst into delighted laughter. "Heavens, it's nothing to worry about," Mrs. Rockaway continued. "She knows she has to be in bed by ten-thirty. I imagine she'll find someone else to corner until then. But she does have an overpowering crush on you, Jimmy, so try not to brush her off entirely, all right? By the way, I see you still have the same excellent taste in young ladies. Ah, someone else has just arrived. Will you excuse me?"

As June Rockaway breezed off caroling another "Da-ahling", Boehm turned sheepishly to Hollinger. "Sally is the Rockaways' thirteen-year-old daughter," he said, having just that moment recalled the information.

Hollinger nodded. "Give her a few years and the whole world will be eating out of her hand. She already has the makings of a natural beauty, and if she's inherited even half of her mother's personality, look out."

"I quite agree." Suddenly there was a tall, distinguished-looking man standing at Boehm's elbow, wearing a charcoal gray and silver pinstripe suit. His hair and mustache had to be prematurely gray, for his face was unlined and there was the twinkle of youth in his clear blue eyes. Boehm conducted a rapid mental scan of all the descriptions he'd memorized, but this fellow wasn't among them. Almost instantly the scientist relaxed.

He was in the presence of a stranger. And if Hollinger had never met the man, then Boehm didn't have to follow a script.

Smiling, Boehm extended his hand. "I don't think we've met, Mister...?"

"Oberer," the man replied. "Roger Oberer. I'm the newest member of the board of Remstock Financial Services."

Even though the name meant absolutely nothing to him, Boehm tried to look knowing. "Oh."

"I came over just now to get a rumor confirmed," Oberer continued.

"Oh?" said Boehm.

"The pundits on Bay Street are predicting that your company is about to close a merger that'll shake us all to the very roots. There's some speculation that you're even using your personal fortune to anchor it."

"Oh?" Boehm hadn't an inkling of what this chap was talking about. At his side, Hollinger grinned mischievously.

"Okay," Oberer sighed. "Since you obviously intend to keep this firmly under your hat until the *fait* is *accompli* –"

Finally, Hollinger spoke up. "Jimmy," he cooed, "you promised there would be no shoptalk while we were on vacation. Can't you two discuss something else for a while and just enjoy the party?"

Boehm turned and smiled a question at Oberer.

After a moment's hesitation, the other man visibly relaxed. "Sure," he said, returning the smile, "why not?"

In a general conversation that he could occasionally steer to the margins of popular science, it was soon obvious that Garrick Boehm was well able to hold his own. So well, in fact, that Hollinger began to feel restless. He decided to leave Boehm with Oberer and do some mingling.

The room they were in was awesomely large; and while its

huge dimensions weren't exactly lost on him, it happened to be one of many such salons that James Hollinger had had occasion to visit. In the circles in which he customarily moved, marble floors and ornate ceilings were the rule rather than the exception. Hollinger had reached the point where he enjoyed spacious surroundings, elegant furniture, and original works of art without being particularly conscious of them. People, however, fascinated him.

All his life, James Hollinger had been a student of people; he couldn't help noticing that there seemed to be an entire school of them, drifting through the salon and library and great room of the mansion as though swept by an invisible tide.

And so he strolled around the room, smiling pleasantly, joining conversations when invited, giving his assumed name when asked, and watching and listening and constantly making mental notes.

Suddenly, Hollinger found himself standing in front of a large, simply-framed pen-and-ink drawing representing a map of the city as it must have appeared around the turn of the twentieth century. It was a quaint reproduction, with important buildings actually drawn in miniature, rather than being depicted as shaded outlines, as later became the practice. Intrigued, he stepped up for a closer look.

The city hall was physically at the center of the town in those days. Distributed equidistantly around it were the university, the port and customs office, and the main post office. In fact, he mused, if lines were drawn joining those three locations they'd form a triangle, with the city hall somewhere in the middle...

Hollinger caught his breath with a shrill gasp. "Oh, my God," he breathed, "that's the answer." Whirling excitedly, he looked for Boehm. The scientist hadn't budged from his conversation with Roger Oberer. Hollinger made his way purposefully across the room, trying not to attract too much attention by hurrying. Once at Boehm's side, however, he tugged urgently at his arm and blurted, "We have to leave."

"What?" Boehm said, startled. "But I was just—"

"It's an emergency," Hollinger insisted, his voice trembling with suppressed excitement. "I'm sorry to have to take him away like this, Mr. Oberer."

"I'm sorry too," said Oberer, perplexed. "What's the matter? Aren't you feeling well? I'm sure our hostess wouldn't object to your lying down in one of the bedrooms—"

"I appreciate your kind offer, but I— it isn't me," Hollinger stammered. Then, turning to Boehm, he added beseechingly, "Please, Jimmy, I really have to go home. Right now."

Boehm was flabbergasted. James had drilled him so insistently on protocol – when to arrive, the earliest they could leave, how and to whom to say goodbye when they did leave, even how much they could eat. He'd put the scientist in terror of inadvertently committing a grievous social gaffe and possibly ruining Hollinger's career. And now here was Hollinger himself, tossing the entire litany out the window and insisting that they depart immediately. It was a lot to swallow. However, since the urgency was obviously genuine, there was nothing to do but follow James's lead.

"I guess I'd better take her home," he said reluctantly to Oberer. "Do you see Mrs. Rockaway? I'll have to make my apologies to her."

"Don't worry about it," Oberer assured him. "June and I are old friends. I'll explain that an emergency forced you to leave early. I'm sure she'll understand."

The butler was happy to call a taxicab for them. It arrived so quickly that Boehm suspected the driver had been waiting just around the corner. As soon as they were inside the vehicle and rolling down to the street, Hollinger leaned forward and instructed the driver to stop at a gas station.

Struggling to fathom this suddenly irrational behavior, Boehm demanded resentfully, "Are you crazy? What for?"

The taxi driver was only slightly more polite. "I've already got a full tank, lady."

"It's not to gas up," Hollinger insisted. "We have to pick up a map of the city." And turning to Boehm he went on excitedly, "I know how we can locate the source of our problem. We triangulate ourselves."

Thoroughly perplexed, Boehm shook his head. "You're not making sense."

"Never mind. I'll have to get a map and show you...."

* * * * *

"You're a dummy, Claire – a prize dummy." Claire had been sitting motionless on the sofa in Boehm's darkened apartment and muttering these disgusted words to herself for almost an hour now. How ridiculous to be so frightened of a phone call or a knock at the door!

After all, Sophie Hopper was a civilized person. Claire's precautions had been exaggerated and pointless. Feeling very silly indeed, she got to her feet and padded over to the tall floor lamp in the living room. But just as she was reaching for the switch, there came a gentle tapping at the apartment door that froze her outstretched arm.

All at once her thoughts began to race. That definitely wasn't Sophie. Sophie's knock would have been much more aggressive. And Garry and James wouldn't have bothered to knock, for they both had keys to the apartment. So who could that be at the door?

Slowly, Claire straightened up and made her way noiselessly into the kitchen. In case her direst suspicions were correct, she wanted to be near a supply of weapons. Then she heard a scrabbling sound at the lock, and a sudden chill ran through her entire body.

It was a burglar. And by being stupid enough to sit that long in the dark she'd let him think the apartment was empty. Why, she'd practically invited him in. If she hadn't been paralyzed by fear, Claire would have kicked herself.

It was the slow turning of the doorknob that finally got her moving again. As quietly as she could, she inched the cutlery drawer open and reached inside. Her fingers closed on the wooden handle of a steak knife. Clutching her weapon, she then tiptoed over to the light switch near the kitchen door. The kitchen light was bright enough to illuminate the living room as well. Perhaps that and the element of surprise would drive him off.

Gently, gently, the apartment door swung open and then closed again. Her breath turning to dust in her throat, Claire reached with a trembling hand for the light switch. *I'm a big, tall man,* she reminded herself, *not a short, weak woman. I will stay calm. I will stay calm. As long as I don't scream.*

Steeling herself, she flicked the kitchen light on.

Two people gasped and froze simultaneously. Caught like a fly in a bead of amber by the brightness pouring through the kitchen door was a short, potbellied man wearing jeans and a matching denim shirt. His greasy hair was slicked right back from his face. His eyes were wide and his jaw hung slack with fear and astonishment.

An instant later Claire had recovered sufficiently from her shock to exclaim indignantly, "Mister Rosseau! What the hell are you doing here?"

"I— Well, I— I thought—"

"You thought the apartment was empty and decided to do a little freelance snooping." Claire shifted her grip on the knife and deliberately brought it into view.

"I'm the superintendent of the building," Rosseau squeaked. "It's part of my job to keep track of the tenants. And when only two out of three go out and the place seems empty...for all anyone knows you might be murdered or something. Didja think about that?"

"I think your vigilance would be much more praiseworthy if you weren't being paid so damned much to look the other way," Claire rasped. "What you just did is called breaking and entering. The police frown on it and so do I. I'd advise you to think about *that*. Now get the hell out of my apartment!"

Claire only had to advance a couple of steps with the knife in her hand to send Rosseau scurrying back the way he came, quaking in fear for his life. As the door slammed behind him she heaved a sigh of relief. And then she began to laugh.

Claire was still chuckling to herself twenty minutes later when Hollinger and Boehm stormed through the front door.

"What are you two doing back so soon?" she exclaimed. "Not that I'm unhappy to see you, but I thought—"

"Never mind that," Hollinger snapped, clearing the end table with ruthless efficiency and wrenching it around to face the sofa.

Claire raised an inquiring eyebrow at Boehm, who merely shrugged in reply. Meanwhile, Hollinger had dropped a folded road map on the table and now rushed off into the bedroom, imbued with grim purpose.

"James? What's going on?" Claire demanded.

All that came out of the bedroom was the sound of an apartment being ransacked, so she turned to the scientist and repeated her question in a vaguely threatening tone of voice.

"He says he's going to triangulate us," Boehm sighed. "That's all I know."

"That's nice. And aside from that, how was the party?" Claire asked wryly.

"I don't know. I didn't stay long enough to form an opinion. How has your evening been so far?"

"Rather exciting, actually. I scared off a burglar."

"You *what*?" Boehm cried.

Just then something heavy crashed to the floor in the bedroom.

"Got it!" proclaimed Hollinger.

But Claire and Boehm were by now too involved in a heated discussion to pay much attention to him.

"Well, it was your idea to turn off all the lights and pretend nobody was home," Claire retorted.

"Did he get inside? What did he take?"

"He didn't take a thing. He wasn't more than a couple of feet past the door when I grabbed the steak knife and confronted him and—"

"Good Lord!" Pasty-faced, Boehm grasped the back of the sofa for support before asking tightly, "Was anybody hurt?"

Hollinger burst from the bedroom into the middle of this dramatic tableau but ignored it, being too preoccupied with unfolding the map on the end table. Without a word, he began drawing bold lines with a ruler and the stub of a soft pencil.

"Nobody was hurt," replied Claire. "But I was sure glad to be wearing your body, I'll tell you."

"Well, *I'm* not glad you were," Boehm snapped. "What if this burglar had been armed with a knife himself, or carrying a gun?"

"Then I wouldn't have shown myself. I'm not stupid, you know," was Claire's irritated response. "But as soon as I saw that it was only Rosseau—"

Boehm was aghast. "Rosseau broke into the apartment? Rosseau, the superintendent? Oh, my God, what next? I can't stay in a building where the super steals from the tenants."

"He didn't come to steal, I'm certain of it," Claire assured him. "I think he just came to snoop around, maybe lift a souvenir or two that he could sell back to us at some outrageous price later on. Rosseau's a weasel, Garry. He goes in for extortion and blackmail because he hasn't the stomach for grand larceny. Now, would you please calm down?" she pleaded. "You're making me nervous."

"Aha!" Hollinger crowed suddenly, startling them both. "What's on the southeast corner of Bloor and Parliament?"

"Hell, I don't know," snapped Boehm. And, finally taking notice of what Hollinger was doing, Claire and Boehm turned and stared over his shoulder at the map. "That area is colored green," Boehm pointed out. "It has to be some kind of a park."

"I think it's a playground," said Claire. "What about it?"

Grinning smugly, Hollinger dropped the pencil stub beside the map and leaned back into the sofa. "Whatever switched us around the other night is located in that park."

Claire nearly choked swallowing a laugh. "James, as weird as our current situation is, I doubt that it could have been perpetrated by a sandbox, a slide and a set of swings. How did you figure this out, anyway?"

"I made our three apartments the vertices of a triangle and then joined them to—"

"Of course!" Boehm smacked a hand to his forehead. "Well, at least we know where you went wrong. I wasn't here when the change took place."

"That's right," Claire chimed in. "I woke up in a building situated... here." And, picking up the pencil stub, she marked the block with an 'x'. All at once Hollinger found himself muscled out of the way as Boehm and Claire took over the map, redrawing the triangle and joining all three vertices to the mid-points of the opposite sides to discover its exact center.

"There," said Boehm with some satisfaction when they were done. "Whatever switched us around is located at the southwest corner of Bloor Street and Avenue Road."

The changelings fell silent for a moment.

"Garry," Claire pointed out reluctantly. "That's the ROM."

"The ROM?" he echoed. "As in Royal Ontario Museum?"

She nodded. "The same. And not the same. It's undergoing a huge renovation right now. Part of it is being torn down. Some exhibits have been moved, others have simply been packed up and put into storage. Searching for something in that chaos is going to be nearly impossible."

"Then we mustn't waste any time," he told her, his voice rising with excitement. "We'd better get over there right away."

"Relax, Garry," she said. "It's after hours. And anyway, I've got a better idea."

Hollinger had just had the same thought. "The Internet."

Working quickly, Claire brought her laptop into the living room and plugged it in. "Since we can't go to the ROM tonight anyway, why don't we see what's on their web site? If nothing else, it'll kill some time."

A few moments later, she had accessed a wireless network and the computer screen was filled with choices.

"Good grief," murmured Boehm. "Egyptian Exhibit, Hall of Minerals, the Bat Cave... There's so much here. Where do we start?"

"We can probably eliminate the Bat Cave," said Hollinger. "Unless you think the culprit might be a Transylvanian count...?"

"Not funny, James," Claire muttered. She slid the finger-pointing icon across the screen and clicked on *What's New at the ROM*. "Hold on, this looks promising – 'New Finds from Middle Eastern Dig'." *Click.* She scanned the repainted screen. "Well, it's not really an exhibit, but some of the pieces are currently on display," she told them. "And they've posted detailed information about one artifact in particular, which means it's really unusual. We're in the neighborhood anyway – want to have a look?"

Without waiting for an answer, she clicked on the word *Demonai*.

There were pages of text about the little statue. Claire scrolled through them slowly, so the other two changelings could read over her shoulder.

"Prostitutes and concubines?" Hollinger remarked. "Well, this is interesting, but not especially useful. Let's move on."

"I don't know about that," countered Boehm, beginning to smile. "We're in genie-in-a-bottle territory here. According to this mythology, Demonai traded favors. You know, some ancient peoples believed that deities could be enslaved – trapped inside containers and forced to grant wishes."

Hollinger opened his mouth to utter a sarcastic comment, then thought better of it. Wasn't that exactly the way he'd been feeling lately – trapped and tapped?

"Hey, look at this," urged Claire, pointing at the color plate of the statue on the screen. She clicked on a button beside the image and a mischievously grinning face appeared on the figure's head. "Maybe there really is a little god inside this thing."

"And maybe you're both letting your imaginations run away with you," Hollinger said disgustedly.

"Come on, James, loosen up," Claire told him. "There's no harm in having a little fun."

"Lady and gentleman, I'm beginning to formulate a theory," Boehm announced.

"Yeah? Based on what?" challenged Hollinger.

"Based on the fact that I did make a wish, the afternoon before the switch, and got exactly what I asked for. I'll bet that if you search your memories, you'll find that sometime that day, you made wishes too, and they've been granted. Maybe not in the way that you expected, but—"

"That's crap!" Hollinger declared. "I never made any wish."

"I did," said Claire wonderingly, "now that I think about it. Two days ago I was trying to force my way through a writer's block, and I realized that what I really needed was to step out of my daily routine and have an adventure. And if this isn't an adventure, I don't know what is. What was your wish, Garry?"

"I wished I could trade places with a rich and powerful man."

"Come on, James," Claire coaxed, becoming more and more excited. "You must have wished for something. Or thought about how great it would be to have something, or do something. Or even just wondered what it would be like…?"

"Nope," said Hollinger firmly. "Not a damned thing."

Claire and Boehm exchanged a look. "Well, you've got something to wish for now," she told him, bouncing off the sofa and onto her feet. "Keep this image of Demonai on the screen, Garry."

"What are you going to do?" he asked.

"Desperate times call for desperate measures. I'm going to find some candles and light them. Then we're going to have a little ceremony to butter up Demonai, and ask him to put us back in our own bodies."

"You can't be serious," Hollinger said.

"Hey, what would be the harm?" she demanded. "I'm in a mood to hedge all my bets. If Demonai is for real, then maybe he'll grant our wish. If he isn't, at least we'll have tried, and all it will have cost us is a little time. You have to learn to go with the flow, James. That's what people do who aren't in control of every situation. And in case you haven't noticed…?"

Hollinger blew out a sigh. "All right. I guess it makes about as much sense as anything else we've done the last few days."

* * * * *

I had nothing to do with this, Demonai declared. *It was all their own idea.*

Really? What about that map on the wall at the gathering place, the one that gave them the information they needed to locate your likeness?

What about it, Aggregator? That map has been hanging there for a while. It was a happy coincidence that the threedee noticed it and was able to make a connection between the drawing and his predicament. In fact, that's the way many problems get solved in the three-dimensional world.

And you can truthfully say that you did not cause the map to appear just at the moment when it would be needed?

I can, Aggregator.

But Olla'set was not convinced – his demeanor remained challenging.

Tillah reminded him, *The threedees are about to gather some trappings and go through a ritual, to ask Demonai to put them back the way they were. Doesn't that prove something, Aggregator?*

They haven't reached any conclusions, he pointed out. *They're guessing. And they're desperate enough to try anything, even a ritual that none of them actually believes in.*

But they can't perceive that their essences are melded, so guesses are all they can make, argued Demonai. *And if they guess correctly, I need to let them know. It's how these creatures learn, by trial and error.*

It's part of the experiment, Tillah chimed in. *You did state that the integrity of the experiment had to be preserved, Aggregator. So far it is proceeding exactly as Demonai planned it.*

Olla'set's essence went still, but he did not withdraw from the meld. *So you are saying that the subjects of this experiment are expected to learn something from it as well? When did you decide to tack this on, Demonai?*

When you threatened to destroy the bubble, Aggregator. These beings may need some time to prove to you that they are, indeed, sentient. I didn't want the experiment to conclude before that happened.

An honest response. How refreshing. All right, then, I rescind my earlier decision. If these creatures cannot prove their sentience, I will not immediately disaggregate them. However, I will reclaim the bubble as my property and return it to my collection sac.

And if they are able to demonstrate sentience, Aggregator?

In that unlikely event, you may decide what to do with the bubble.

What about the wishes? Tillah wanted to know. *The threedees are going to ask Demonai to put them back the way they were. And he does need to let them know they've guessed correctly about the source of their problem.*

You can give them one hint, Demonai, warned Olla'set. *After that they have to figure things out on their own.*

CHAPTER EIGHTEEN

2003

Still March 17, 9:45 p.m.

Across the street, two men sat in the dark in a late-model sedan, watching shadows flow and sway behind curtained windows on the second floor of Boehm's building.

"You're sure these guys are holding that millionaire?"

"Yep. Augie got it from Gunther, and Gunther knows better than to lie." The second man rolled his window down and pitched a cigarette butt out onto the street.

"Bruno! What did we talk about earlier?" scolded the driver.

"Sorry." Hurriedly, the first man got out of the car and retrieved the butt.

"Jeez! It's a filthy habit to start with, but if you're going to litter the streets—"

"Y'know something, Dougie? Ever since you got that job with Waste Management, you haven't exactly been a barrel of laughs. I picked up the damned butt. Now shut up about it, and keep your eyes on those windows."

"It doesn't look like much is happening up there, Bruno," the other man remarked after a moment. "You're sure he's still alive?"

"He was alive when the broad shoved him into the cab at that other rich guy's house, and he was alive when she pulled him out of the cab at this address. Augie said the guy didn't look very happy. But whether he's alive right now, I don't know."

"We oughta go in there and bust him out."

"Dougie, Dougie, Dougie," said Bruno in a sad, singsong

voice. "We're not in that line of work anymore, remember? Bustin' in on people is against the law. So if Augie says to sit and watch the house, that's what we do."

"But what if they kill the guy while we're sitting out here?"

"They won't. Stop and think. They don't have a car, not even a rental. So they obviously aren't pros, but they're not stupid either. If they decide to do him, they'll call a cab and take him to an industrial part of town. Then they'll make him walk, at least a mile, to somewhere private. A quarry... an abandoned factory...l ike that. And we'll be right on their tail. Those were Augie's orders."

The driver sighed. It was going to be a long night.

* * * * *

Boehm was having another of those dreams. The three of them were kneeling at the foot of a huge faceless statue, a ring of candles burning around them. Claire held her laptop aloft, a finger poised to hit the delete key. She prayed to Demonai in a strange tongue. Sang him songs. Made extravagant promises. Sudden fear struck deep into Boehm's heart. What were they doing here? Demonai had been trapped in that statue for centuries. What terrible vengeance might he wreak once they had released him?

"Claire – no!"

All at once...he was one hand clapping...he was hot buttered popcorn...he was old tennis shoes...he was one second too late. The key had been pressed, the pin had been pulled, his fate had been sealed. On the statue's blank face, the features of Demonai slowly appeared. They puckered and twisted, as though he were struggling to speak. At last, the huge crystalline lips parted – and Demonai stuck his tongue out at them, and laughed.

The laughter took shape and grew larger and larger. It attacked and swallowed Boehm, surrounding him like a huge soap bubble, turning and tumbling him and pushing Claire and James out of his dream altogether. And it grew, and stretched, and finally burst, with a short, shrill scream that sounded as though it was right beside his ear. Then it screamed again, and again, pushing even Boehm out of his dream...

It was the telephone. What the hell was it doing beside him? Hollinger's voice couldn't answer the phone, especially not at this hour of the night. Wait a minute, he was in the bedroom. Did that mean—?

The phone screamed again. To put it out of his misery, Boehm reached over and fumbled the receiver off its hook. "Hello," he croaked.

"Garry, is that you?" sobbed a female voice.

"Of course, it is," he said, shaking his head to clear it.

"You've got to help me, Garry! I think I've killed a man."

"You're not sure?" Who *was* this woman?

"I'm afraid to roll him over to check his heartbeat," she whimpered.

"Mm— What about the pulse in his neck, the carotid artery?" Gradually, Boehm's thoughts were sorting themselves out.

"I don't even want to touch him."

"Well, what did you do to him?"

"The same thing I did to you, remember? Only he's hit his head on something and hasn't moved in almost five minutes and— I'm scared, Garry! Please, come over," she pleaded tearfully.

So he was back in his own body, being asked to help dispose of another body. Well, why not? This would probably turn out to be a dream anyway... "Okay, okay," he muttered. "Where are you?" She gave him an address in the Beaches which sounded vaguely familiar. He hung up and immediately dialed for a cab, his excitement growing.

Claire wasn't the only one who could have an adventure.

* * * * *

The corpse was groaning and shaking his head. Boehm saw

him briefly through the open doorway as he arrived on the scene. Then his full attention was taken up by the tall redheaded beauty who stood across the tiny purple room in a most engaging state of undress. She was gnawing her knuckles and staring with green eyes wide as traffic lights at something around the level of Boehm's knees. Fortunately, he thought to look down, or he might have tripped over the obscenely-perfumed lump of masculinity clinging soddenly to the floor.

"Is he going to be all right?" she whispered anxiously.

"I don't know," said Boehm. "Let's ask him. Will you be all right, sir?"

"Mmmphgblmmnn," replied the corpse.

"Come on, fella," Boehm sighed, and hoisted him to his feet. "Well, he looks a little the worse for wear, but your friend will probably live..."

Instantly, the temperature in the room dropped several degrees. "He isn't my friend," she informed him. "He came pounding at the door at some ungodly hour, practically forced his way in. I'd never seen the creep before in my life. And where the hell do you get off making an assumption like that?" she demanded, hands on her hips.

Boehm wasn't sure how to reply. Suddenly ill at ease, he turned his attention to the would-be midnight cowboy who sagged like a tired pillow in his grasp. "There's a cab waiting. I'd better get this guy down to the street," he muttered, and half-dragged, half-carried the dazed intruder over to the stairs.

Meanwhile, Sophie exhaled sharply and sank down onto the bed. What did it take to get a rise out of that man? she wondered. Was she losing her touch? Or was this handsome scientist truly as ingenuous as he acted? He knew from first-hand experience how she discouraged unwanted masculine attentions. Surely he must have realized that she was also perfectly capable of disposing of unwelcome nighttime visitors, that the midnight phone call to his apartment had been nothing more than a ploy?

Apparently not, she mused. If Garrick Boehm had shown even a speck of jealousy she would have noticed it. Sophie glanced briefly at the corner where her flannel granny gown still lay, rolled up in the ball she'd made of it after changing into Claire's baby dolls. They were a very tight fit on her, but that was all right. Sophie had been determined to look sexy for Boehm when he arrived.

Suddenly it dawned on her: He'd said there was a cab waiting. There was no way she was going to let him just ride off with that groggy pervert!

* * * * *

The two men sitting in the parked car across the street from the rooming house became suddenly attentive when they saw the front door open.

"See, Bruno?" Dougie crowed, poking his partner in the ribs. "Who says you can't put a stiff into the back seat of a cab?"

"I see him. But he looks too short and fat to be our millionaire."

"So what's the hit man doing all the way out here?"

"That," said Bruno, pointing.

A woman wearing next to nothing had appeared in the doorway and was now beckoning to the man to return inside.

"Hubba, hubba," murmured Dougie, awe-struck. "He's got a girlfriend."

"Girlfriend, wife, whatever – she's his weakness, and we're going to keep an eye on her."

"What about the other broad? She's still holding that Hollinger fella."

Bruno uttered a frustrated syllable. "This is getting too damned complicated. Gimme the cell phone. We'd better call Augie."

* * * * *

Although of two minds about returning to the purple room

upstairs, Boehm finally gave in to a carnal impulse and headed back into the building, quaking at the thought of his own foolhardiness even as his feet eagerly negotiated the three flights of wooden steps.

The redhead had resumed the pose she'd struck just before his stammering exit with her victim several minutes earlier. Hands on her hips, bosom thrust forward, chin jutting, she stood glowering at the doorway as he stepped through it. Boehm could feel a lump growing in his throat...and something else growing farther down.

The amazon took a slow, deep, magnificent breath. "Has anyone ever told you what a gorgeous hunk of man you are, Garry Boehm?" she demanded fiercely.

Now his mind was reeling. *This is a dream*, he told himself. *It's only a dream. There's no need to panic.*

"You do feel the same way about me, don't you, darling?" The apple-green pajama top plastered itself to her bosom as she swept across the tiny room, closed the door and took him in her arms. Then, planting her mouth on his, she gave him a kiss that he could feel all the way down to his ankles.

So this was today's woman? he thought hazily. Hurray for today's woman...

She yanked the bedcovers down with businesslike efficiency, then turned on a smile that threatened to melt him into a quivering mass of goose-flesh. Together they set about removing his clothes.

Roxanne hadn't really been his first, he suddenly realized. She'd just made love to Hollinger's body, with Boehm's mind along for the ride. This time, he was in his own body. This time, he was going to lose his virginity for real.

To a warrior princess.

"Oh, yeah, baby!"

* * * * *

If Boehm had thought he could return unnoticed to the

apartment, he was mistaken. All the lights were blazing as he walked through the door. The other two changelings, in slippers and robes, were waiting impatiently in the living room. When he paused on the threshold, debating the wisdom of coming inside, Hollinger strode over and yanked him in, slamming the door behind him.

"You're awake," Boehm observed brightly.

"Phone rings in the middle of the night, I wake up in the wrong body, and you go sneaking off somewhere and come crawling home at dawn with a peculiar air of contentment," spat Hollinger, "and it surprises you that we're not both sound asleep?"

"Wait a minute – wrong body? You're in your own body. Aren't you?"

"Nope," said 'Hollinger', jerking a thumb in the direction of Claire's body. "And neither is he. Demonai must like you, Garry."

"So where were you?" demanded James.

After a moment's hesitation, Boehm decided to tell the truth. "I was with a woman," he stammered. "She phoned here, all in a flap. Something about a man in her apartment. She was afraid she'd killed him."

"Yeah, right," said Claire.

Suddenly Hollinger inhaled sharply. "Oh, my God! I meant to tell you, but in the rush to get the cocktail dress and make it to the party it completely slipped my mind. Ralph Ignace. He wanted to pay you for the story as soon as possible. He insisted on delivering the cheque personally to your apartment."

"But I'm not at my apartment," Claire pointed out, still scowling.

"That's right," Hollinger agreed. "Sophie is."

Two pairs of eyes widened simultaneously, then turned in amazement to focus on Garry Boehm.

"Sophie killed Ralph Ignace?" Claire's voice was a horrified whisper.

"No, he's fine. A little groggy after hitting his head. I put him into a cab and sent him home. Then I went back upstairs to check on Sophie, to make sure she was all right."

"And?"

"She was better than all right," Boehm said with a grin, his face the color of a well-cooked lobster.

To Claire's great annoyance, Hollinger burst into laughter.

CHAPTER NINETEEN

2003

March 18, 11:50 a.m.

"See? What did I tell you?" It was Bruno's turn to crow, although after spending the entire night and most of the morning on surveillance, his voice was a little gravelly. "She's the magnet, and he's the iron filings."

"That's a big building," Dougie pointed out uncertainly. "One of us should have followed her inside, Bruno. She could be in any one of those apartments right now."

"Don't you worry about that. Augie's working on it."

"I thought he was watching the other place."

"He called while you were taking a leak. Hollinger and the broad left together right after blondie did. Augie followed them to a diner, where he says they're having lunch together, sociable as you please." A worried pause, then, "Y'know what I think, Dougie? I think the kidnapping was a scam. I think Hollinger and the short broad are working together, and blondie is the guy we ought to be worrying about."

"*Now* can we bust in on them?"

"Yeah, soon as Augie gets us a location for the redhead."

* * * * *

Sophie was conducting a last-minute inspection of her living room. Crimson lips pursed, she glanced around at the gold and white French provincial sofa and easy chair, the martini pitcher sitting on her great-aunt Hilda's heirloom silver tray in the middle of the freshly-polished walnut coffee table, the tasteful arrangement of artificial flowers that crowned her antique magazine rack. Sophie had suggested to Boehm before they'd parted early that morning that they meet at her apartment for an intimate cocktail or two and perhaps lunch. After all, now that they were friends, what further reason could there be to prolong her stay in Claire's hideous little purple room? He'd accepted the invitation with endearingly boyish eagerness, and she had packed up her things and rushed back home to set the place in order before he arrived.

The furniture had been dusted and the martinis had been mixed. She'd slipped into something alluring and done her face and nails. He would be arriving momentarily. Her excitement rising, Sophie searched the room for anything she might have missed, but all was in readiness. There were even two shrimp cocktails thawing on the kitchen counter.

Just then the doorbell rang. She gave a final pat to her halo of flaming hair before hastening to answer the chime.

Boehm lounged against the door-frame in a devil-may-care pose he'd once seen in a magazine illustration. "Hi there, gorgeous," he said, his voice tremulous with suppressed excitement.

Sophie ran one manicured hand suggestively over the edge of the half-opened door. "Hello," she replied with a smile. "Why don't you come inside and get comfortable?" And she nudged the door fully open with one exquisitely rounded hip.

The sight and smell of her were making Boehm lightheaded with anticipation. This was no longer a dream for him — it was a dream come true. A beautiful woman in a sexy dress was inviting him into her apartment. And there was a smouldering expression in her eyes that left no doubt whatever about her intentions. It was a brand new and very heady sensation, being considered a sex objcct. Boehm was determined to enjoy every second of it.

"Care for a drink?" she offered, gesturing negligently toward the martini pitcher on the coffee table.

Not trusting his voice, he just nodded.

Next thing he knew, they were sitting side by side on the sofa, sharing a conspiratorial smile.

"To us," she whispered, delicately touching the rim of her glass to his.

All at once...he was chocolate custard...he was a mosquito looking for a snack...

"No!"

"Garry, what's wrong?"

Tentatively, Boehm glanced around him. He was in the arms of a beautiful redheaded woman in a flimsy pale green dress which had crept nearly a foot above her knees. She was lusting after his body almost as much as he lusted after hers. What could possibly be wrong?

"Uh, nothing," he reassured her with a feeble smile. *Except Demonai might be having second thoughts about me.*

* * * * *

What was THAT?

Demonai had to wait for the crashing waves of sensation to subside before he could even attempt to answer Tillah's question. *The lamp – someone's rubbing it.*

It was probably Richard Slattery, summoning him to talk to the Russell boy. His timing stank.

Suddenly, another huge breaker swept through Demonai, powerful enough to ignite sympathetic energy bursts in the threedees' essence meld. The pleasure was so intense that it devoured every other feeling, blocked all conscious thought. For a moment, Demonai himself ceased to be, as electrical spasms whirled from one end of him to the other. Then, at last, the storm of sensation weakened and died.

Demonai forced himself to manifest satisfaction.

That is truly disgusting, remarked Olla'set. And yet, his pod remained melded to those of Demonai and Tillah. *Can't you do something about it?*

You're only saying that because you've never experienced such pure sensation, Demonai replied. *It's a shame. You've missed out on so much... pleasure.*

Is that what you choose to call it? Olla'set retorted. *Because it doesn't appear to me as though you're enjoying yourself, Demonai. Quite the opposite, in fact.*

Olla'set is right, Tillah chimed in. *It feels as though you're being tortured, Demonai. It's that lamp, isn't it? You need to pull your pod out of it immediately.*

I can't. Slattery needs to be able to contact me and this is the only way he knows.

Then you need to find out who is rubbing the lamp and tell them to stop, said Olla'set. *Do it right now or I'll do it for you.*

CHAPTER TWENTY

1998

March 25, 11:35 a.m.

There was only one person in the dean's study, and it wasn't Richard Slattery. It was a female, short and plump, with her dark hair knotted into a bun at the nape of her neck. She was wearing a blue shirt-waist dress and a white apron, and she had just set the lamp – his lamp – carefully on a piece of newspaper on Slattery's desk. Curious, Demonai watched her use a white cloth to scrape up a blob of something gray and gelatinous from the bottom of a wide-mouthed jar labeled Tarnish-Off. As she grasped the lamp firmly with one hand, Demonai felt a shiver race through him and decided to nip this one in the bud, so to speak.

Let go of me!

The maid screamed and yanked her hand away from the lamp as though it had just sprouted teeth and tried to bite her finger. At the same time, the cloth she'd been holding took flight, landing blob-side down in the middle of Slattery's expensive Persian carpet. Her eyes wide as saucers, she stood transfixed, staring in horror at the lamp. Her lips were working, although no words were coming out; and she began touching herself lightly and rapidly with the fingertips of her right hand, in a repeating pattern: forehead, chest, left shoulder, right shoulder, forehead, chest, left shoulder, right shoulder.

This was interesting. Demonai wondered what else he could make her do.

Who said you could polish me? he demanded.

Slowly her face crumpled, and she burst into tears and raced for the door, shrieking and waving her arms. At the threshold, she ran right into Richard Slattery, who was coming the other way.

"Flora, what's wrong?" he demanded, bobbing and weaving around her, his arms outstretched at his sides.

Bemused, Demonai watched them do their strange little dance in the doorway to the study. Twenty-eight years earlier, Slattery would have simply grabbed this hysterical woman and immobilized her against his chest. Now, he had to worry about being brought up on charges if he so much as laid a finger on her. Life in the threedee world had become very complex indeed.

"*Signor* Slattery, the lamp! It is possessed! I clean. I try to polish – it *speak* to me! It is a devil lamp, *signor*, a devil lamp!" wailed the maid.

Abruptly, Slattery stopped moving as his expression morphed from concern to dread. "You tried to polish that lamp?"

She nodded energetically.

He sighed and shook his head. "Demonai," he muttered.

"*Si, si!*" she shrilled. "A devil!"

"Flora, I'll take care of this. Why don't you go work upstairs for a while?"

Stealing frightened glances over her shoulder, she let him persuade her toward the stairs. When she was safely on her way to the second floor, Slattery strode into the study and closed the door behind him.

"Demonai, that wasn't very kind," he said sternly, addressing his reproach to the lamp, which was, admittedly, a lot cleaner now than it had been a short while earlier. It lay on its side as though waiting to be gift-wrapped in the newspaper.

And it was the height of consideration, I suppose, to put the librarian's car upside down in a tree...?

Slattery breathed a sigh... of regret? Or was it nostalgia?

"That was a long time ago, D."

Yeah, tempus fugit, I get that. Nonetheless, you shouldn't have left my lamp sitting around where someone might get the urge to polish it, Ricky. That *wasn't very kind – or very smart, for that matter – unless you* wanted *me to scare the living daylights out of that woman...?*

Slattery's spine snapped erect, completely belying the expression of resignation on his face. "You're right, Demonai. You're absolutely right. I'm sorry about the false alarm. I'll tuck the lamp away so this can't happen again."

CHAPTER TWENTY-ONE

2003

March 18, 11:50 a.m.

It was an unprepossessing little diner, about five blocks from Boehm's apartment. The menu was severely limited, as was the seating – ten on swivel stools at the snack bar and about as many again at the several tiny tables that stood against the outside wall; but the change of surroundings had acted like a tonic on Hollinger and Claire's mood. The tablecloth, which the waitress had spread for them after taking their orders, was washable plastic with a cheerful red and white striped pattern that matched absolutely nothing else in the place. The flatware was plain-handled and, to Hollinger's surprise, sparkling clean. Skimpy paper serviettes came one at a time from an institutional metal dispenser at their elbows. Considering how far off the beaten track they were, or perhaps because of it, the service and food were remarkably good, Claire thought.

"How's your chili?" asked Hollinger, gesturing idly with a forkful of tuna casserole he'd detoured temporarily on its way to his mouth.

"Delicious. Can't you see the steam coming out of your ears?" she replied with a mischievous smile. "I'm glad we came here instead of rattling around the apartment all day."

He nodded agreement.

Sitting there, aware of her own eyes gazing intensely into her face, Claire suddenly felt a flush of heat that owed nothing to her spicy lunch. "So," she managed to say around her mouthful of chili, "tell me your theory."

"My theory?"

"To explain why Garry and I got switched again and you didn't."

He shrugged. "I don't have a theory."

"I think maybe I do. You were the only one of us who denied making a wish the day the big change happened, remember? So when we asked Demonai last night to consider our wishes granted and put us back—"

"Claire, we were looking at an image on a computer screen. If Demonai even exists, and that's a very big 'if', I doubt whether he has an online presence."

"Nonetheless, he heard us, James. And he returned Garry to his own body. Maybe we ought to be asking ourselves why Garry's request was answered and ours weren't. Garry's original wish was to change places with a very rich and powerful man. Do you happen to know why?"

"He said it was because he'd been thrown out of a job when the government funding was cut for a research project he was working on. He was feeling poor and powerless, and I guess he thought having lots of money would make him feel better."

"But it didn't."

"Nope. And it didn't help when he discovered there was a downside to being James A. Hollinger. It made him really angry."

"James, don't take this the wrong way, but I got the impression that the only thing he didn't like about being in your body was the fact that you insisted on micromanaging it."

"No, I didn't."

"Yes, you did. You couldn't do anything about the fact that he had your physical body – which you repeatedly reminded him was only on loan – but you made damn sure he couldn't use your money, and that kept him from exercising your power. It's no wonder he resented you, James. You prevented him from getting his wish."

As realization broke over Hollinger, Claire was treated to the sight of her own body sagging into its chair like a deflating blow-up doll. "Son of a bitch... I had no idea. So now that you're the one occupying my body..."

"...am I going to get on your case about your hiding your credit cards? No. I never wished for money or power, James. I wished for an adventure, and that's exactly what I got. And what about you? Are you still going to deny that you made a wish?"

Hollinger sighed. "I wanted to turn back the clock. I wished that I were back in my twenties."

"So Demonai put you into a more youthful body – mine."

"If he exists – and I am not yet ready to concede that he does – Demonai didn't just put me into a more youthful body. He put me into a female body. I don't call that granting a wish, Claire. I call that playing a dirty trick."

"Well, according to the write-up on the web site, that's par for the course for Demonai."

"Oh, please!"

Claire gasped as a sudden thought occurred to her. "Wait a minute, James. That could be it. I wished for an adventure I could write up for the glossy magazines, like winning the lottery or visiting the penguins in Antarctica. Instead, I've got a story that nobody in his right mind would believe. You wished for youth and got a gender change along with it. Garry wished for wealth and power but in your body he wasn't able to use any of it. I think we've all three of us been pranked by the trickster god."

Claire leaned forward and would have said more, but, all at once... they were ham and eggs... they were a cerebral hemorrhage... they were a bad case of acne....

* * * * *

Demonai! Again?

I can't help it. Anytime a threedee touches or moves the lamp I get a surge of energy. It will subside.

Meanwhile, it's raising sympathetic sparks in the threedees' meld and destabilizing it. Olla'set could decide that the experiment is being compromised.

Be patient, Tillah. Don't let him withdraw his pod from the bubble. The experiment is succeeding on more than one level, and I don't want our aggregator to miss any of it.

* * * * *

Claire was holding a forkful of tuna casserole in one hand and a slice of buttered bread in the other, and was sitting across a tiny table from a tall man with thinning dark hair and startled eyes.

"Oh, my God," she breathed after a moment's shocked silence. "It's really happened, hasn't it?"

Hollinger took a deep breath. "It looks that way. I wonder how long Demonai will let us stay ourselves."

"So you believe in him now?"

"I'm still reserving judgement on that."

"Well, whether he exists or not, I think we should drink a toast to being back in our own bodies," she declared, reaching across the table for her glass of diet ginger ale.

Half-convinced, he picked up his cola. But just as they touched the rims of their glasses lightly together...

... they were peaches and cream... they were Mutt and Jeff... they were measles....

Muttering imprecations under her breath, Claire flung her fork into her bowl of chili as Hollinger leaned back in his chair with a discouraged sigh.

"Maybe there's more to this than just figuring out whodunit," said Claire.

"What more could there be? Howdunit? Good luck with that."

She shook her head. "Maybe whydunit. After all, there are nearly three million people in this city, all making random wishes every day. So why us? What made our wishes so special that

Demonai decided to grant them in a way that linked up our lives?"

Hollinger chuckled to himself, prompting Claire to ask, "What?"

"Demonai, if he exists, is supposedly the patron deity of prostitutes and concubines, right?"

"Ye-es..."

"I moonlight as a tax return service for half the strippers in this city. You're a good writer, Claire, but you're forced to pay your bills by editing porn."

"And Garry?"

"When scientific research depends for its existence on the generosity of government bureaucrats, mightn't that be seen as prostitution?"

"I'm sorry, James, but I just don't see how you fit the definition. Strippers aren't prostitutes *or* concubines, and you're a successful financial analyst. I can't even imagine you being forced to demean yourself just to keep food on your table and a roof over your head."

"I wasn't always a successful financial analyst. Some of the things I had to do to get my business off the ground would have— Never mind. Tell me more about your wish."

"I wished for an adventure because I've been living hand-to-mouth for the last three and a half years," she told him. "I figured if I wrote a first-person article about doing something that most people only dreamed about, the piece would sell for sure to a major publication, and— Don't look at me like that, James. Toronto is an expensive place to live."

"So when you asked for an adventure you were actually wishing for money."

"I guess I was. And we know Garry was wishing for power. And you were wishing for...?"

"Sex," he replied uncomfortably after a pause. "I wanted to be younger so I'd get laid. A lot."

"You're joking," she exclaimed. "Garry said he woke up in your body, in bed with a very attractive blonde."

"Roxanne. Once a year, for a couple of weeks. And I do her taxes. It isn't the same thing."

"Oh, really?" Claire cocked her head, raised an eyebrow and said, "If I didn't know better, I'd say you had a concubine, Mr. Hollinger. Demonai is the special protector of concubines. So I think we need to consider the possibility that he may have been listening to four wishes that day, not three."

The heart-shaped face went pale.

Claire leaned forward confidentially. "Tell me about her, James. When did you first meet her?"

"Is this really necessary?" he demanded impatiently. "Fine. I met Roxanne twenty years ago, when she was a stripper at the Brass and Feathers Club. She wanted to know how to quit stripping without losing any income. I told her to use her savings to buy into the club and phase herself off the stage."

"Did she take your advice?"

"Apparently. She currently owns fifty percent of the place. Makes a tidy sum."

"And once a year, when you do her taxes, she comes to the penthouse and has sex with you. How often?"

"Claire!"

But she refused to back off. "For two weeks you're a couple. How many times on average during those two weeks do you make love?"

"Once or twice a day. What exactly is your point, Claire?"

"Let's just run this one up the flagpole. You see, I wished for money and an adventure because I didn't have any of either one. And Garry wished for money and power for the same reason. But you had what you wanted right under your nose – you just didn't realize it. You're the roadblock here, James. Garry's part in this is done. But my adventure can't end until Demonai is able to put us *both* back into our own bodies."

* * * * *

... he was a bat in a belfry... he was a banana cream pie...

He was quivering like a plucked string.

Sophie was halfway out of her dress, her nipples rising in hard little cones. Boehm should have felt warm; instead, he was breaking out in a cold sweat.

"Garry, what's the matter?"

"I think I need to go to the ROM."

"The museum? Now? Why?" she asked, frowning with concern.

"To pray..."

* * * * *

All right, conceded Olla'set, reluctantly rejoining the meld. *So they're intelligent and they share information. And guesses.*

Demonai was too busy to reply. The ferocious current of sensation had begun coursing through him again. Every part of him was sparking. What in the name of the Universe was happening to that lamp?

Demonai, they're doing it! said Tillah. *They're thinking their way through their situation, just as you predicted they would. Demonai, are you all right?*

CHAPTER TWENTY-TWO

1998

March 27, 4:15 p.m.

"Hello, Mac."

O'Toole had been expecting this call. It was the logical next step in the elaborate April Fool's joke that Paulina Perrone had set in motion in his office four days earlier. Slattery hadn't lost his touch – his voice on the phone sounded taut and a little ragged, just as though he were being harassed night and day by Olla'set the Magnificent.

"Rick," he acknowledged. "How have you been?"

"I've been better, my friend. I'm actually calling to invite you to a small gathering at my home this evening at eight o'clock. Just five or six... people."

The hesitation caught O'Toole's attention.

"Oh? What's the occasion?"

"There's someone I'm ready for you to meet. Remember all those practical jokes we pulled off when we were at law school?"

"You mean those jokes *you* pulled off, without telling me how you did it."

"I had help, Mac."

"That much I was able to guess."

"I know it's short notice, but he'll be here tonight. Can you make it?" There was an unspoken 'please' at the end of that question that intrigued O'Toole while at the same time putting him on his guard.

"This is interesting timing, Rick. Should I wear armor?"

"Mac, trust me, this is not an April Fool's joke. I wish it were, but— You'll understand when you get here. If you're coming, that is."

O'Toole debated with himself for a moment, but curiosity won out. "Okay, I'll be there," he said, certain that if this did turn out to be a joke, at least it would be a damned ingenious one.

*****

O'Toole surrendered his topcoat to the manservant who had opened the door to admit him to the Slattery family mansion and was shown with great deference into the drawing room. He'd often been a guest here while he and Rick were school mates. The old-money elegance evident in the quality and style of the décor had greatly impressed him those thirty years ago. Now Rick lived here alone, attended by a butler, a cook and a handful of maids, and Mac didn't know whether to feel sad or relieved that nothing about the house seemed to have changed.

Rick got to his feet and walked over to shake O'Toole's hand. "Thank you for coming, Chief Magistrate."

The use of his title cued Mac to look for others in the room, and he soon found them, sitting goggle-eyed in two of the brown leather loungers arranged around the fieldstone fireplace. As he'd expected, this 'meeting' was part of the joke.

Paulina Perrone leaped out of her chair as though propelled by a spring the instant their eyes met. The young man made a *pro forma* effort – the cast on his leg made the gesture of respect impossible. O'Toole sorted through his repertoire of expressions and finally settled on his pronouncement-of-sentence face as he acknowledged each of them in turn. "Ms Perrone…and this must be Mr. Russell."

"It's an honor to meet you, sir," said the plaintiff as Paulina sank back down in her seat.

"Dean Slattery," said O'Toole, remaining in character as he

returned his attention to the chief perpetrator of the prank. "When do I get to meet the genie?"

Rick's shoulders sagged. "Please have a seat, Mac. I have a story to tell you, one you'll find very difficult to believe."

CHAPTER TWENTY-THREE

2003

March 18, 12:45 p.m.

"Darling," breathed Sophie, "what's the matter? Your hands are shaking."

Boehm gazed up at her unclad loveliness and smiled weakly. "It's all your fault," he murmured, pulling her down on top of him again just as...

... he was a rotten tomato... he was a charcoal briquet...

... he was getting tired of the whole damned thing.

Suddenly there came a vigorous pounding at Sophie's apartment door.

"Open up!" commanded a deep voice. "Don't make us break the door down, lady."

"Don't you call me 'lady'," she muttered darkly. "Garry, I'm sorry about this." Sophie covered herself with a silky blue dressing gown and strode into the living room.

Boehm raised himself lazily on his elbows and enjoyed her exit.

A moment later, Sophie opened her apartment door to two burly men in business suits.

"Are you Sophie Hooper?" one of them demanded.

"Hopper," she corrected him frostily. "Who the hell are you?"

"Where's your friend?" the other man wanted to know.

"I've got lots of friends," she replied. "You'll have to be more specific."

"Don't try snowing us, Miss Hooper. We know what you've been up to," snapped the first man. "Where's your partner?"

With as much dignity as she could muster in the presence of two strange men who 'knew what she'd been up to', Sophie drew herself up, looked her accuser straight in the eye and demanded, "Since when is that a crime?"

"Conspiracy has always been a crime, Miss Hooper," he replied, gesturing quickly to his companion. Suddenly they shoved her backward and burst through the doorway.

"Ee-*yah!*"

The first man went flying and slid into a heap behind the antique magazine rack.

"Ee-*yah!*"

His partner's body described an arc in the air and made a perfect landing on Sophie's French provincial sofa. There was a sharp crack as he touched down.

Boehm waited for the commotion to subside before making an appearance in the living room. As he came through the bedroom door, Sophie whirled on him. "Garry, I know you're in some kind of trouble, and I'm on your side, but I can't help you if you won't talk to me. You were expecting these two to come after you, weren't you? That's why you were so distracted this morning."

Running a hand through his hair, Boehm sighed and shook his head. "Sophie, I swear to you, I don't know either of these men. I can't even imagine who might have sent them. Maybe we should call the police."

"Okay. But first, help me tie them up," she ordered him. "When they come to, we'll just ask them who they're working for. Then we'll find that person and pound him into the dirt. *Then* we'll call the police."

* * * * *

"Stop hogging the headache pills," Claire groaned. "And stop insisting that we go to the ROM. It won't do any good. Demonai has already heard us; and he's going to keep switching us back and forth until we do whatever it is he wants us to do."

"Or until he reaches the end of his attention span and decides to torture somebody else." Hollinger, now back in his own body, lowered it wearily into the easy chair in Boehm's apartment.

"Why is it so hard for you to accept that Roxanne loves you?" she demanded.

"Do we have to go into this?"

"Yes. You say she makes a tidy income. Boehm says she's a beautiful woman. She's probably had plenty of chances to marry and have kids, but she never did. Instead, she spends two weeks a year pretending to be married to you. Speaking as a woman, I have to tell you that this all adds up to one thing – she would rather have you for just two weeks than have somebody else year-round. And that, my friend, is a pretty damned good definition of love."

"Maybe you're right. But I blew it, Claire," he murmured sadly. "You heard what Garry said. She never wants to see me or hear from me again."

"Until she forgives you. That's what we women do, James. We vent and then we forgive."

"Have *you* forgiven me?"

"Yes, several times, and that's just today. Come on, James. Don't let one little telephone message stand between you and your true love."

"You're planning to turn your adventure into a romance novel, aren't you?"

"I could," she replied with a grin. "There's plenty of material. Garry's on a hot date with Sophie right now. And I'm positive that you and Roxanne can get back together if you'll just take a leap of faith and let her know how you feel about her."

"I've really looked forward to those two weeks every year," he conceded. "And I wouldn't mind spending a lot more time with her. But from the way she talked, I just sort of assumed that two weeks with me was all she wanted."

"Okay, that's a start. So all you have to do now is—"

... they were overripe bananas... they were lightning and thunder...

Not again!

... they were wet socks...

"What the hell do you want?" Hollinger shouted at the ceiling as his body looked on from the chair where he'd left it.

"Maybe I was wrong and it's not all about you," Claire sighed. "Maybe Demonai wants something more from me as well."

"All right, let's see. Do you really like the color purple?" he demanded.

She made a face.

"I'll take that as a no. Here's a tougher question: Are you happy writing and editing porn for a living? I read a few pages of your story on the way to Ralph Ignace's office, and they were good, Claire. Really good."

"Yeah, a lot of people have told me that. I just wish they'd put some money where their opinions were…"

"... Toronto being an expensive place to live," he concluded for her. "So why are you here? Writing's a portable profession. You could have stayed back in...?"

"Caverley Corners. Population 4700. A main street six blocks long. Lots of rolling hills and farmers' fields everywhere else. And five donut shops, all doing a brisk business," she added with a smile.

"And everybody knows everybody else," he continued, "and they look out for one another and just get together and pitch in when something needs doing, right?"

"Not like the big city at all," she agreed.

"And you miss it. Don't you?"

"You know, you're pretty smart for a reformed sexist pig."

"I have a theory."

"Finally!"

"Well, it was my turn. I think Toronto is the reason you're blocked. This place is a big pressure cooker, Claire. Stay here long enough and you'll fall apart."

He was right about one thing. She was what she was, a small town girl still struggling to fit in after three and a half years. As she was opening her mouth to tell him so...

... they were corned beef and cabbage... they were dandelion seeds on the wind...

* * * * *

Demonai had had a plan, he was sure he had, but the crashing waves of sensation had so disturbed his essence that he was hard pressed to remember a single detail of it.

Olla'set, we have to do something. This is killing him.

Demonai brought this upon himself, Tillah. I warned him not to become so involved with the five-dimensional universe, but he ignored me.

It's the lamp. Demonai, withdraw from the lamp!

But he did not respond, and the others were afraid to touch him.

We must communicate with the threedees and get them to stop rubbing the lamp, Tillah decided. *Aggregator, you've communicated with them before. I haven't yet learned how. Please, do this now! We are only three. If Demonai dies, one third of our kind will cease to exist. Is that really what you want?*

CHAPTER TWENTY-FOUR

1998

March 27, 9:05 p.m.

"Give it up, Dean Slattery," said O'Toole wearily. "There is no genie inside the lamp."

"He was there two days ago," Rick insisted. "I don't understand why he isn't responding now, since he was the one who wanted to have this meeting."

"Maybe he didn't like being jostled around in the trunk of your car," O'Toole suggested.

Suddenly a booming voice erupted from the fireplace:
PUT... DOWN... THE LAMP!

Slattery nearly jumped out of his skin. As he hastened to obey the command, he couldn't help noticing that two of his guests had instantly blanched. Joseph Russell was hyperventilating. He looked about to faint.

"That's Olla'set!" hissed Paulina Perrone, casting anxious glances around the room, several of them at the young man resting his leg cast on Slattery's brown leather ottoman.

Meanwhile, O'Toole was leaning farther back in his chair, his arms crossed, his expression skeptical.

Slattery cleared his throat and asked, in the courtroom voice he'd often practiced when he was younger, "Where is Demonai?"

Demonai won't be answering your calls anymore. In fact, he won't be speaking to you at all.

Involuntarily, Slattery shivered. "Is he dead?"

Of course not! Olla'set replied. *He has merely withdrawn from this place.*

Questions were crowding Slattery's mind, but before he could pick one and ask it, Paulina Perrone jumped to her feet, her fists clenched at her sides. "Olla'set!" she cried in the direction of the fireplace. "I represent Joseph Russell, the human you've been tormenting for the last ten years. Before you leave, we need to talk."

Then talk.

"You nearly killed this boy with your bullying and your threats. We want you to forget about your so-called tribute and leave him alone, from now on." And she closed her eyes, as though expecting to be struck down at any second.

Interesting, said Olla'set after a pause, and Slattery could swear he heard a smile in the genie's voice. *I was about to say something very similar to you. Demonai is right – your kind don't frighten easily any more. Very well, then. Joseph Russell, I absolve you of any obligation to provide tribute and promise never to communicate with you again.*

Uttering a sudden impatient syllable, O'Toole stood up and went over to the fireplace. He shot a look at Slattery before bending to inspect the hearth and the flue.

"What are you looking for, Mac?"

"The microphone. Honestly, Rick, I'm a little disappointed. This prank is nowhere near the high standard of mischief that I was expecting from you."

You think you can debunk me? demanded the voice from the fireplace.

"I think there's nothing *to* debunk. A child could have come up with this. In fact, I suspect a child did," O'Toole declared.

Olla'set chuckled, sending icy tingles across the back of Slattery's shoulders. Suddenly, five glowing white orbs appeared in the room. Hovering at chest height, they formed a ring around O'Toole, who stood frozen, his eyes wide with belated comprehension.

"Please, Olla'set, don't disaggregate him!" Slattery cried.

I won't harm him, Ricky, the voice promised. *I'll just give him a lift home. We can talk on the way.*

As the orbs moved in, there was a bright flash of light. A second later, three people sat in Dean Slattery's study, staring in shock into one another's faces. It was a full minute before any of them dared to speak.

"What just happened here?" Paulina asked, her voice barely a whisper. "Is he gone?"

"They both are," said Slattery, finally understanding what Mac had been feeling years earlier when he talked about 'the end of an era'. "I believe you've won your first case, Ms Perrone, although I wouldn't try putting it on my résumé if I were you. And now that I know for sure that it's empty, I can finally polish and display that antique lamp. As for Chief Magistrate O'Toole..."

Right on cue, the telephone rang in the vestibule and was answered by the butler. A moment later, he stepped into the drawing room and said, quite calmly, "That was Mister O'Toole, sir. He told me to convey a message. He says congratulations, and he is sorry he ever doubted you. Also, he requests that you bring his topcoat to your office tomorrow morning so that he can pick it up and congratulate you in person."

And, to the amazement of Paulina Perrone and Joseph Russell, Dean Slattery began to laugh.

* * * * *

All right, Demonai, said Olla'set. *I have observed enough. Your experiment is over. Dissolve the meld and let these creatures get on with their lives.*

Are you convinced of their sentience, Aggregator?
No.
But you communicated with them yourself, protested Demonai. *You have observed that they are self-aware, that they can reason*

and form theories, that they experience emotions and can both plan for the future and remember the past. They learn and evolve. They question and explore. How can you say that they are not sentient?

While it's true that they do display most of the characteristics of sentience, I'm afraid the most important one is missing: the ability to create nonsentient life in lower dimensions.

How is a three-dimensional creature supposed to create life in only one or two dimensions? wondered Tillah.

Exactly. And that is why the Universe only bestows sentience on the highest order of beings. There can be no life in one or two dimensions. Therefore these threedees cannot possibly be sentient.

I disagree, Aggregator, declared Demonai. *They are sentient, and I can prove it.*

CHAPTER TWENTY-FIVE

2003

March 18, 1:50 p.m.

... he was rice pudding with raisins....

Boehm felt the moment pass and resumed breathing. He was still in his own body, thank goodness. And Sophie and the two thugs tied up in her living room were all staring at him curiously.

"Are you quite done now?" Sophie wanted to know.

"Hey, cut the man some slack," scolded one of the thugs. "He isn't well."

"Shut up, Dougie," growled the other man from his seat on the broken sofa.

"Dougie?" mused Sophie. "I'd have guessed you were Felix and Oscar. If you've finished sniping at each other, perhaps you'd be good enough to tell me why you're here."

"It was his idea to bust in here," piped up Dougie.

"Dougie..." warned his partner. Sophie turned and scowled darkly at him.

"Augie just wanted us to watch your place, make sure nobody got killed."

Now she did a double take. "Killed?" she echoed.

"Like that other guy, the one you loaded into the cab."

The thug on the sofa cursed loudly and began thrashing around in his bonds. "Dougie, if you don't shut up right now—!"

"How long have you been following us?" Boehm demanded.

"Ever since you kidnapped the millionaire out of the Ha'penny."

Sophie was mystified. "Garry, what the hell is he talking about?"

But Boehm just stood there, smiling and shaking his head. "Excuse me," he said. "I have to make a phone call."

* * * * *

"What do you think?" Claire wondered. "Was that it?"

Hollinger looked himself up and down. "Well, we're back in our own bodies, and that's a good thing."

Just then, the telephone began to shrill.

"Oh, Lord," groaned Claire. "And Garry's not here to answer it."

Hollinger crossed the room in two strides and snatched up the receiver. "Hello?" he barked. As Claire watched tensely, he listened for a couple of moments, then smiled and said, "You've got it."

"Well?"

"That was Garry. He wants us to meet him and Sophie at the Ha'penny."

"James, should we be socializing at the pub so soon after—?"

He reached over and pulled her to her feet. "Grab your purse and shake your buns, lady. It isn't a social call. There are a couple of men over there who need some straightening out."

* * * * *

O'Meara nearly had a heart attack when he saw them walk through the door. "Gunther!" he whispered urgently.

"I see them, Ewan. Want me to call my cousin again?"

"It's too late. Here they come."

Hollinger pasted on his most cordial smile. He approached the bar, leaned his elbows on it, and greeted the bartender brightly. "Hi, there. Remember me?"

"Mister Hollinger," said O'Meara warily. "What can I do for you?"

"You know, I want to thank you for trying to protect me the other day. I'm only sorry it wasn't necessary."

"Then you weren't...?" said Gunther.

"No. I was angry and upset, and I probably said a few things that could have been better phrased. But I wasn't being kidnapped. These really are my friends."

O'Meara looked behind him, into three smiling faces. Two of them belonged to the hit squad, and the third was worn by a tall redhead who looked as though she could snap the bartender in half. "Your friends?" he repeated uncertainly.

"Yes. I'd left a note that evening, asking them to meet me here."

"Look, Mister Hollinger, I don't know exactly what's going on, but—"

"I want you to send me the bill for any damage that was done to your establishment as a result of our...misunderstanding," said Hollinger.

Money was something Ewan O'Meara had no difficulty accepting. At last, he relaxed and grinned. "Sure thing, Mister Hollinger. Maybe you and your friends would like to have a drink, on the house."

James straightened up and glanced around. "Maybe another time. I've got some unfinished business to take care of."

"So what do you think, Ewan?" said Gunther as they stood watching Hollinger and his 'friends' stroll back onto the street.

"He was different somehow. I just can't put my finger on it."

"Is he for real?"

"He'd better be," snorted O'Meara. "It's costing me ten grand to put this place back together, and another ten in lost business, and I intend to collect every penny of it."

* * * * *

What is this place, Demonai?

Threedees come here to amuse themselves, Aggregator.

Then where are they? All I see are transportation devices, lined up in rows.

Demonai, observe! said Tillah, sparking with excitement. *On that surface. Aren't those...?*

...two-dimensional creatures which the threedees have made, he confirmed. *Threedees come together in their transportation devices so they can take pleasure in observing the activities of these creations. There are other gathering places as well, inside shelters, where threedees without transportation devices can go.*

Doesn't this prove they are sentient, Aggregator? Aggregator?

Very interesting, remarked Olla'set. *These twodees appear to be indestructible. After disaggregation they are able to reaggregate themselves and continue their activity. And some of them are very strangely made.*

Have you seen enough, Aggregator?

Not yet, Tillah. Be patient. I wish to observe some more.

CHAPTER TWENTY-SIX

2003

March 18, 8:25 p.m.

There was a solemn air in Boehm's apartment, a sense of closure, of finality. Packed luggage littered the living room. For days, they'd been forced to coexist, and now that the bond was broken and they were free to go their separate ways, none of them really wanted to leave.

"I wish I could have gotten to know you both much better," said Boehm.

"You still can, Garry. You do remember where I live?" teased Hollinger.

"Gentlemen, it's been an adventure," declared Claire.

Boehm agreed emphatically, "It certainly has." He slipped an arm around Sophie's waist and pulled her closer to ask, "So what now?"

"Now you take me shopping for another sofa, sweetie," she told him, not missing a beat. "One that won't break when a man's body falls onto it."

Claire looked from one to the other of them. "Dare I ask?"

Sophie just turned and winked at her.

"Well, I hate to break up the party, but I have to return to the penthouse to make a very important phone call," said Hollinger, reaching for his suitcase.

Thinking of Roger Oberer, Boehm remarked, "Merger proposal?"

Hollinger grinned at him. "You might say that."

"Sophie," said Claire, "I think you should know that I've decided to move out of the rooming house."

"Finally!" declared the redhead. "Do you have another place lined up?"

"Caverley Corners. I'm going back home."

"To write your novel? Good for you." Sophie gave her a hug. "Be happy, be sure to invite us to your book launch - and don't forget Women for Professional Equity."

Involuntarily, Claire recalled the last meeting of that organization that she had attended, and shuddered. Forget Women for Professional Equity? Not in a million freaking years.

* * * * *

These twodees are definitely not sentient, Olla'set declared. *They keep performing the same activities over and over, in exactly the same way.*

And the threedees, Aggregator? Demonai wanted to know. *Are you finally convinced of their sentience?*

As reluctant as I am to relinquish an object that has afforded me so much pleasure, I am forced to agree with you, Demonai. I'm not sure why the Universe chose them to receive such a gift, but I cannot deny the evidence. The threedees are sentient. The bubble is yours to dispose of.

Mine to study, Aggregator. Yours and Tillah's to share and enjoy with me. After all, we're gods now. We can't just abandon the beings under our protection.

Gods of what, Demonai? asked Olla'set. *And who are we protecting?*

Olla'set was asking questions. An excellent beginning, Demonai thought.

We protect whomever we wish, Aggregator. Like all sentient beings, we have choices.

EPILOGUE

2014

June 27, 10:15 p.m.

The door opened on the third knock.

"Please, I know it's late, but I didn't know where else we could go."

The shelter worker standing in the lighted doorway glanced down at the little girl, no more than five or six years old, clutching a well-loved Raggedy Ann doll with one hand and her mother's skirt with the other. Then she met the other woman's pleading gaze and smiled.

"You're in the right place. Come in, quickly."

"We have nothing," the woman continued, tears in her voice as she stepped over the threshold. "I'm sorry, I should have packed a suitcase, but— I really thought he'd changed. Then, this evening—" In the hallway the shelter worker took a closer look at the woman's face. There was a fresh bruise on her cheek, and her chin was streaked with blood from a split lip.

"He just went crazy. There wasn't time for me to do more than grab Shelley and run. If he hadn't tripped and fallen on the stairs while chasing us we wouldn't have gotten away at all."

"Well, you're safe now," the shelter worker assured her. "We have a room where you and Shelley can sleep tonight. Tomorrow we'll take care of the rest."

"It's going to be all right, Mommy," piped up the little girl. "Just like my dolly said."

The shelter worker got down on one knee, putting her face at the child's eye level, and smiled warmly at her. "She's a pretty dolly, Shelley. And she can talk?"

"She talks to me when I'm by myself."

"Shelley hasn't let that doll out of her sight since her grandmother gave it to her last Christmas," the woman explained.

"I see," said the shelter worker, still kneeling. Then, speaking to the child, she asked, "And what's your dolly's name?"

"Tillah. She's my sidekick."

ABOUT THE AUTHOR

Born and raised in Toronto, Arlene F. Marks found her muse at the age of 6 and has been writing and sharing her stories ever since. Her dual passions are teaching and writing, and she has indulged them both liberally over the years, chalking up numerous professional writing and editing credits in both fiction and nonfiction fields between stints in the high school classroom. Most recently, she is the author of *From First Word to Last: The Craft of Writing Popular Fiction* (2013, Legacy Books Press) and the LITERACY: MADE FOR ALL series (2014, Rowman & Littlefield Education) as well as *The Accidental God*. She is currently at work on a series of novels set at the turn of the 25th century.

Arlene lives with her husband on the shore of Nottawasaga Bay and welcomes visitors to her web site:
www.thewritersnest.ca

Made in the USA
Charleston, SC
24 April 2015